Praise for *Comedic Timing*

"People who've been 'that woman crying on the subway just after moving to New York' will feel so seen. (It's me. I'm people.) *Comedic Timing* is a raw depiction of romance and friendship, featuring all the complexity of navigating sex and love as a bi woman."

—Kate Goldbeck, author of *You, Again*

"I've never read a story that so deftly captures the beauty and overwhelm of expansive attraction. Sexy, profound, and deliciously funny, *Comedic Timing* plunges us into the exhilaration and terror that comes along when you try something—or someone—new."

—Haley Jakobson, author of *Old Enough*, a *NYT* Editors' Choice

Comedic Timing

UPASNA BARATH

831 STORIES

831 Stories
An imprint of Authors Equity
1123 Broadway, Suite 1008
New York, New York 10010

Copyright © 2025 by Upasna Barath

Cover design by C47.
Book design by Scribe Inc.

This is a work of fiction. Names, characters, places and incidents either
are products of the author's imagination or are used fictitiously.

Library of Congress Control Number: 2024947631
Print ISBN 9798893310276
Ebook ISBN 9798893310238

Printed in the United States of America
First printing

www.831stories.com
www.authorsequity.com

For Mom, who insists my flaws
only make me more lovable

Comedic Timing

I

Armed with a bottle of red wine, I approach a stranger's home seeking a clean slate. No one at this party knows me. No one has an opinion on my breakup, barely a month old. No one needs to choose sides. I left Chicago, and I live in New York now—even if it's only been two days.

I arrive at a brownstone in Bed-Stuy. I try the buzzer and wait for five minutes, chilly in the cool air of a September evening. A breeze brushes against me, raising the hairs on my exposed limbs. I should have worn layers. I double-check my hair with my phone camera before calling someone named Christian, who I'd been put in touch with via text. He appears and prances down the steps, his hair even blonder than in his photos on social media. He greets me with a bear hug.

"Naina," he says into my shoulder, as if we're childhood friends who haven't seen each other in years. "So good to meet you."

"Nice to meet you too," I respond, laughing at his easygoing familiarity, the yeasty smell of beer on his breath. "Jordan says hi. I brought wine."

"Pshhh, you didn't have to," he says, taking the bottle. "Come on inside."

The distant hum of traffic gives way to the typical sound of some party, somewhere: voices and music, muffled and thumping above the creaky staircase Christian gestures for me to climb.

We approach the apartment door, and he swings it open to reveal a duplex space. Bodies are bathed in moody, atmospheric lighting. My chest pulses with bass. I have never been inside such a spacious, and likely expensive, apartment. There's an ultramodern, bulbous-looking couch dominating the living room and a hand-knotted rug—the kind my mother would have fawned over—at its center. There are a half dozen people sitting on the ground, holding red wine in an assortment of mismatched glassware.

Compared to most of the other guests, my outfit feels both too formal and yet insufficient: a little black dress. Everyone's looks are curated with the right mix of outdated (presumably thrifted) pieces—scarves, wide-leg pants, sparkly tops—and newer ones, evidence of an understanding, or at least an acceptance, of the importance of fashion. These are the kind of people who sit on nice furniture while sipping wine out of repurposed jars.

People flow in and out from the balcony. Cigarette smoke floats over their heads and into the apartment. I suddenly feel very small, or perhaps just very young, momentarily regressing to a meekness I haven't felt since I graduated college three years ago.

Christian smiles at me assuredly.

"I live here with two roommates," he explains. "Rana and my friend David, who you missed singing 'Happy Birthday' to."

"Oh no," I respond. "I love singing 'Happy Birthday' to strangers."

"I'll introduce you when I find him," Christian says. "Want some cake?"

In the kitchen, Christian and I squeeze past a group of friends wheezing with laughter. Christian was right—the wine was unnecessary. The kitchen counter is chock-full of bottles and empty beer cans indistinguishable from half-drunk ones.

He opens mine anyway. "Sorry, don't know where all the glasses are," he says, rifling through cabinets. From the counter, I pick up a red Solo cup with the name "Margot" written on it in black Sharpie. "Don't worry, Margot left me hers," I say. Christian snorts, grabbing the cup to rinse it before serving me a generous pour.

"Your apartment is very cool," I say.

"Thanks," he says. "It's changed a lot. We've been living here for seven years, almost."

"Whoa," I respond. "That's commitment."

"In one area of my life," he says, shrugging.

Christian digs a vape out from his pocket—hot pink, like some kind of toy—and offers me a hit. I take it and inhale, even though I don't really vape, and I know it's terrible for you.

"Trying to quit," he says, as if reading my mind.

"Remind me how you know Jordan?" I ask, referring

3

to my best friend who introduced us and promised that we'd get along.

"I met him at a mutual friend's comedy show. I *hooked up* with said mutual friend," Christian adds with a drop of pride, as if announcing he'd won an award. "And I debriefed with him. I didn't know who else to talk to about it. Been pals ever since."

"That's sweet. I love my morning-after debriefs with Jordan," I respond, hoping to conceal the very real sadness I feel from missing my friend. Our postmortems would feel different now with eight hundred miles between us.

"How do you know Jordan?"

"College," I reply.

"Are you in comedy, too?"

"No. I could never," I reply. I don't mean for this to come off as derogatory, so I add, "But I respect it. And most of my friends are comedians."

Christian squints cynically at my comment and continues: "Has anyone ever told you that you shouldn't be friends with comedians?" He laughs, grabbing a bottle of beer from the fridge. He digs a set of keys from his pocket, looking down to find what he needs, and pops the cap swiftly.

"Mostly that I shouldn't date them," I say. "But I really do laugh more because of Jordan. I'm a writer, to answer your next question."

"That's cool. Is that what you do for money?" He sips his beer as if testing it, then tilts the bottle back for more.

I try not to look crestfallen at this involuntary reminder

of my reality. I clear my throat. "For money I work in marketing."

"Ah." Christian nods.

"One day, you know, I hope to write for money."

"Totally. So, what do you write?"

I gulp my wine. I haven't had to talk about this yet in this new city. I don't know how it will feel. "Mostly satirical essays. Commentary on internet culture." I turn the question back to him. "So what do you do for money?"

"I work as a software engineer," he says, grimacing. "But I tell people I'm a comedian because that's what I am. I used to be in an improv group in college. That's how I met my roommates." He tilts the bottle back again, filling his cheeks with the liquid before swallowing.

"What do they do?"

"David's a filmmaker," Christian explains. "Well, I mean, for money, he's a video editor. My other roommate, Rana, is a social worker."

A woman enters the kitchen and places her hand on the back of Christian's neck. "Speak of the devil," Christian says. Without addressing me, Rana asks for his vape, securing it before swiftly exiting the room.

"Please know that outside of this context, I'm not inhaling from an adult pacifier every five minutes," Christian says. "I just really wanted it for the party."

"What's going on there?" I ask Christian, gesturing toward the strange, flirtatious dynamic between him and his roommate.

"Oh no. Rana has a boyfriend," he says. "She's just

really affectionate when she's drunk. And on Molly. She's on Molly."

"Ah."

"We've hooked up before, but no—just friends. And roommates."

"Oh, the old lovers-to-friends-to-roommates pipeline," I say.

"What about you? You single?"

I steady myself to respond neutrally. "I just broke up with my girlfriend. Incidentally, she's also a software engineer."

"How boring," he says, grinning and nudging me with his elbow. We already have an in-joke.

"But I applied for a job here, just to see if I'd get it. I did, so I moved. I just wanted a fresh start. I've been here for a few days now."

"Well, are you okay? Since the breakup?"

"Not really. But I will be soon, don't worry."

"Well, yeah. I can tell you're the dumper, not the dumpee." He gulps more beer and swallows a burp.

I consider clarifying that even though I did the breaking up, I don't feel like I came out on top. All my and Sofia's mutual friends are checking in on her, while I have been turned into the villain. I only have Jordan to confide in. Sofia is clearly the more sympathetic person in this situation. Defending myself would do nothing to change that.

I tell Christian to go play host—it's not his responsibility to entertain me—and after my third and decidedly last cup of wine, I run into the Margot who I suspect belongs to the cup I commandeered. She drunkenly introduces herself by pointing at it with her mouth open. "You're a Margot?" she asks, shouting over the music, pushing a wisp of blond hair away from her face.

"Whoa. Freaky," I say. "We look alike, too."

She blinks, then bursts into laughter.

"No, not a Margot. I'm Naina," I say. "I stole your cup."

"I thought you were for real!" she exclaims. "I'm pathologically gullible."

We find ourselves on the balcony with Margot's friend, who sports a mullet, discussing dating deal-breakers: Mullet says he could never date someone who can't handle spicy food. Margot tells him to get his priorities straight. Christian joins, passing a joint, and when it makes its way to me, I take a baby hit.

"Want to come upstairs?" Christian asks me, his head cocked to the side. Margot raises her eyebrows and looks away, as if to pretend she can't hear us. "The drug room," Mullet states ominously, his voice dropping an octave. I ask if they're joining. Margot shakes her head, evading eye contact with Christian.

Mullet waves goodbye, like a princess. "'Twas a pleasure," he sings.

"Margot's a stand-up comic, but she's not that funny," Christian whispers to me as we climb the stairs.

I roll my eyes. "You sound jealous," I say, poking him. "Comedians are so competitive. What's the story there?"

"Margot is an old friend. It's not my business to share, but Margot and David—my other roommate?—were together for two years. We were all friends, then they started dating, and it got messy."

"This is why I don't get dating apps," I say. "Why download them to meet up with a stranger when you can just corrupt the dynamics of your friend group?"

When we make it to the upstairs room, I'm stoned, and my body feels the tug of the queen-size bed. I climb atop it with a few strangers.

"How long were you together?" Christian asks, squeezing himself in next to me. "You and your girlfriend?"

"We met when I was nineteen," I say. "She's five years older."

"How many people have you dated?"

"That was my only relationship ever."

"Wow," Christian says, weirdly in awe.

He looks at a text message on his phone. I wonder if I'm boring him. "Be right back, duty calls," he says. When he leaves, I turn my attention to a stack of books sitting on top of a patched-up fireplace, a mix of self-help and American classics. Next to me, a woman snorts a line of something off a small tray. We make eye contact as she gently rubs her nose.

"Hey," she says.

"Hi. Oh, I like your eyeshadow. Blue. Nice." *Awkward.*

She dabs at her nostrils with her ring finger. "Thanks, girl. Want some?"

"Coke?" I ask. She nods.

"Oh," I respond, weirdly embarrassed. I am tempted to snort a line despite never having snorted anything. I am suspicious of my urge to let loose, wondering if it is a good or bad thing. I shake my head, forcing myself not to look away as her blotting turns to vehement wiping.

The door swings open with sitcom flair, drawing everyone's attention. A tall man steps in, and they all slowly break into "Happy Birthday." "It ended two hours ago," he replies as he gestures for calm, his arms moving in gentle, measured arcs. "I'm here to use my bathroom, don't mind me." David, Christian's roommate. He smiles at everyone with a quiet magnetism, the kind that makes a person instantly likable without effort. My eyes scan him, catching on the thick hair that curls around his ears, his sharp jaw, the strain of his shoulders against the cotton of his shirt. I assume he's used to being the most attractive person in the room by default.

"Want some?" the cocaine girl asks him. He grimaces, revealing a few crooked bottom teeth. "Did you test that?" he asks. She shrugs.

"Don't shrug at me!" David teases. "I'm not judging you. Just be safe. We have test strips in the kitchen drawer downstairs, for future reference."

"So you don't want any?" she asks him. David shakes his head.

"Aw come on. You used to be fun," she replies.

"Are you peer pressuring me?" he jokes. She shrugs again. I can't tell if they're flirting, but something about their interaction makes me uncomfortable enough to want to interrupt.

"He's right," I chime in. "Why not just test it?"

David's eyes find mine, and I meet his gaze, noticing a boyish sincerity etched in his expression. He suddenly turns self-conscious, brushing something off his shirt, white and crisp like he ironed it. His bicep flexes subtly.

"See?" he says, gesturing to me with his thumb. "You hear her?" The woman rolls her eyes at us and leaves the room, either to get the strips or to escape the conversation.

David turns to me, smiling and squinting. His eyes crinkle mischievously. "Can you believe that?" he asks. "So cavalier."

"I know, right?" I reply, laughing.

"I haven't seen you before, have I?" he asks, his gaze shifting over me.

"No, you haven't," I reply. "Unless you're mistaking me for some other brown woman!" I poke him in his shoulder playfully, but it lands flat. *What made me say that?*

He pulls his chin in. "Why would I do that? I'm brown."

"I see that. What kind of brown are you?" I ask, crossing my arms. *Oh, good, I am making it worse.*

He lets out a single laugh, *ha*. "That's pretty racist, you know."

I fake a scoff, relieved to have him playing along. "Not racist."

"What's your name?" he asks.

"Naina," I say as I hold out my hand. "Thanks for having me. Christian invited me."

He takes my hand, and we exchange what is not so much of a handshake as a brief handhold. It's less a greeting and more an excuse to touch the other person. We might both be guilty of making it that way. I feel his calluses press against my palm. He finally releases his grip.

"I'm David."

"Happy birthday," I tell him. My brain is on a lag, I realize. My wrist is still extended in his direction. I force my hand down, hoping my mind will catch up. "How old are we?"

"Thirty-two."

"You don't look a day over twenty-seven," I reply. David snorts.

"Thanks. Christian didn't mention he was seeing anyone," he says.

"Um, no, we're not—I just got out of a breakup. And then I moved here. From Chicago." I've repeated a variation of this explanation so many times tonight. This time it comes out in a string of breathless words. *Why am I desperate to let him know I am single and definitely not dating Christian?*

"So, you ran away," he says, curling his lip teasingly. In a sense, he's correct, but I won't tell him that.

"Actually, I got a job here."

"Congrats. That's great news. Except maybe not so much for your ex-boyfriend."

"Ex-girlfriend."

David pulls his chin in again, this time out of surprise. "Huh."

"What?"

"I wouldn't have guessed," he responds with a shrug.

I'm confused, not sure what to make of this statement. *He wouldn't have guessed what?* He looks me up and down quickly, as if trying to solve something. I turn self-conscious, feeling trapped in the fucking LBD. The dress accentuates my femmeness, my D-cup breasts, the curve of my waist that my mother deemed part of my "lovely figure." It suddenly feels too short, this dress that previously sat untouched at the back of my closet for years. Tonight, however, it had made its way into a first impression by virtue of being one of the least rumpled things to emerge from my moving boxes.

To this man, me being queer is a surprise because of the way I look. Blood rushes to my face, igniting a silent fury.

His face turns concerned. "What?"

"Do you usually just go around making assumptions about people's sexuality?" I ask tersely.

The energy between us twists. He covers his face. His nails are short, as if bitten.

"I'm . . . very sorry. That's not what I—that was stupid," he says through nervous laughter. "I didn't mean it that way; I wasn't thinking."

I blink at him, wondering what he could have meant other than *You don't look queer to me.*

I cross my arms, and he cups my elbows, his face softening as mine hardens. "Can we start over?" he asks, his voice quieter. "But I *really* need to pee, so let me do that first. Don't go anywhere."

He disappears into the bathroom. The coke girl returns, test strips in hand, waving them at me as if to say *See?!* I want to wait for David, at least to hear his version of "starting over," but wearing this outfit, meeting these people, and being out in this world has turned from novel to unbearable. I crave the comfort of being alone, with myself: of peeling the dress off my body, scrubbing the city off my face, and crawling under my duvet, naked.

I walk downstairs and gently push myself through a group of people dancing to a Mischief song I loved in high school. I hold my breath against a wicked mix of stale cigarettes and strong perfume. I pause to look for Christian, to say goodbye, but I give up after one scan of the crowd.

Determined to escape, I shove open the apartment door and jog down the stairs of the building, landing on the balls of my feet. I step into the cool air of the night, mood lighting now swapped for the dim fluorescence of streetlamps.

I fidget with the hem of my dress, as if stretching it down will somehow make it grow longer. In all my time living in Chicago, I never did drugs, despite Jordan's penchant for microdosing shrooms at birthday parties. I rarely drank more than I could handle. But I also wasn't comfortable meeting new people, and I didn't always speak my mind. Substances aside—my Irish exit aside—I had fun tonight. I surprised myself.

I could see my life in New York as an opportunity to do something I'd never done before: It was an opportunity to grow. As I wait for a car to take me home, I give myself permission to try.

II

Monday morning, Jordan video calls me and asks about the party. I'm waiting in line to order a bagel and coffee, along with a few other people, all of us preoccupied with our phones. Jordan, insistent that Christian is hot, turns our conversation into a friendly argument.

"He's like a golden retriever," I say. "Adorable but kind of stinky and clumsy. There's nothing hot about that."

"*I'd* fuck him," Jordan says confidently. I laugh.

"He's hot," he insists. "Don't pretend he's not hot."

"He's not attractive to me," I say, my eyes darting around defensively, surveilling for eavesdroppers.

"Because he has a penis?"

"Genitalia has nothing to do with it," I whisper, shielding my voice with my hair as best I can.

"Oh, fair enough," Jordan says. "I still remember you drunk making out with that sexy Republican guy in college." Now Jordan is grinding coffee beans in the background. I have a burst of longing for my life in Chicago, for the morning debriefs that didn't have to take place through a screen. When he would make me a mug of pour-over, too, and get coffee sludge all over his kitchen counter.

"Thanks, Jordan. That's definitely one of my fondest memories. Also, I don't know if 'sexy' and 'Republican' go together."

"They *can* go together, and you're so welcome. Did you meet anyone else? Anyone interesting?"

"Sure. I talked to a bunch of people," I say, thinking of David, how quickly our conversation had turned from flirtatious and lighthearted to sour and combative—at least on my end. "I'm still wondering if I should . . . branch out," I say before I put my bagel order in.

"I *told* you. You don't want to hang out with comedians. Especially the New York ones."

"I have to meet people somehow. Plus, they're not all comedians. I think."

Jordan snaps his fingers. "*Oh*, remember Tanya? We went to college with her? I think she lives in New York now. You should reach out."

"Tanya the influencer who takes mirror selfies while on the toilet for makeup sponsorships?"

"I thought that photo was very chic."

As I shove my breakfast into my tote, I deliberate bringing up David. Not mentioning him makes him matter more, I decide. And I know Jordan will be honest with me and tell me if I overreacted.

I step out onto the street, juggling my coffee, my bag, my phone. "So, there was this guy at the party. He seemed nice at first. We were talking, kind of bantering. Flirting,

I think. But then he put his foot in his mouth and felt so bad he found me on Instagram the next morning and messaged me to apologize."

"No way. What did he say at the party?"

I relay the story to Jordan, who replies, "You're upset because he was flirting with you?"

"Be serious, Jordan. What he said was really offensive."

"It's not that bad. He probably wasn't thinking. You take things too personally!" I know he's right, at least partially; David unknowingly struck a spot that was raw for me, even after all these years of growing confidently into my queerness.

"So, what did he say in his message?" Jordan asks. "And what's his name?"

"David. He apologized, said he was offensive, then invited me to Christian's solo show this weekend."

A car honks. A truck blasts its horn in response. Jordan is silent. "You there?" I ask.

"Naina," he says, his voice dripping with giddiness. "I think I found his Instagram."

"Whose?"

"David Azarbad? That's him?"

"Jordan."

"You didn't say he was *sexy*. And he's a Virgo!"

I roll my eyes.

"This is exciting for you!" Jordan exclaims. "Listen, you should accept his apology and become really good friends with him. Then you can introduce *me* when I visit."

"You want me to befriend a hot guy just so you can meet him?"

"Oh, so you think he's hot," Jordan pokes. I laugh, grateful that Jordan can't see me shrugging.

"I have to go. I have my first day of work."

"Best of luck! Happy new job!"

"You make it sound like a threat."

"I'm sick," my new roommate Jhanaki says, pulling a mask over her face as I walk into our apartment after my first day at work. "I left the office early." She has a nasty cold. She tested for COVID twice. Negative. I admire her commitment.

"Can I get you something? Some soup?" I offer, not really wanting to go back out again but knowing it's the appropriate gesture.

She shakes her head. "Thank you. My mom dropped some stuff off. Along with too many kinds of medicine." Jhanaki falls into a coughing spell, making eye contact with me helplessly between phlegmy bursts.

She is a Queens native and is talkative, in an anxious way. Even when we met over a video call, her shoulders seemed energetically glued to her ears. Her nervousness doesn't matter, though. She is intimidatingly stunning—wide, light-brown eyes, pronounced cheekbones, shampoo-commercial hair that flows down across her shoulders—and this is more unnerving than her chattiness. She works in finance and rarely seems to be home, given early mornings and late nights. When she is around, she sits in front of the fifty-inch screen in our living room and watches reality TV—wealthy women arguing over plans canceled last minute, British people making out in hot tubs.

Her sick routine and her well routine look pretty much the same: her on the couch. "Well, that's nice of your mom," I finally say, feeling tender. "I miss my mom's cooking. She is no longer with us," I add, trying not to sound too sad. *With us*. I never know the most gentle way to put it. Jhanaki's features go flat, like she doesn't know what to say. "I'm sorry, Naina," she replies, a softness in her voice due to the coughing or empathy. "I didn't know that."

I am quick to deflect, asking her what she is watching, suddenly feeling vulnerable. I shut my feelings out, irritated at the inconvenience of my emotions.

We spend a few minutes talking—"this show is just teenagers doing drugs and having sex," she explains—before she gathers her blanket and Kleenex to put herself to bed.

"Have some of my food," she insists. "I can't finish it myself. One can only eat so much daal."

I'm embarrassed I said anything about my mother. I shut myself in my room and throw myself on my bed, too, but more as punishment.

Since my move, I have been attempting to fill my newfound free time with writing. I scribble in my journal, thumb words on my phone's Notes app, stare at the blinking cursor in a blank Word document. I want to anchor myself in what I can rely on amidst all the newness: words on a page. Or on a screen. But journaling has quickly become complaining via long-form. I had an idea for an essay, but as soon as I tried to string it together, the phrases came out stilted and rudimentary. At least I can type on my phone with zero pressure, I tell myself. Except most of my missives there are simply sentences I've fished out of my stream of consciousness with no further consideration (*"People who have three or fewer photos on their Instagram profile have my whole heart"*). I wonder if I can blame the breakup, if it drowned out the voice in my head.

I check my phone and reread David's message.

davidazarbad: Hi Naina, it was nice to meet you last night. I didn't get to say goodbye before you left! I want to apologize for what I said. In person, if possible. It was weird and offensive. I swear I'm normal (ish). Let me know if you want to come to Christian's show this Friday. Maybe I'll see you soon.

I know I might have been too hard on him. I could've been more polite and gracious in that moment, more patient and willing to have him learn from his blunder. At the very least, I could have waited to leave until he returned from the bathroom.

I am used to this cycle of reacting and then regretting. I have a tendency to be emotionally impulsive in arguments over seemingly small stuff. I am always subsequently guilty for not being more measured in my responses. Alternatively, I repress my anger over big things only for my emotions to become pressure-cooked. When I started seeing a therapist in college, I worked on unpacking this, but—like many people—I struggle to make my self-awareness useful. To regulate my feelings in real time. To force myself to find the right release valve.

My mother used to coax my wrath out of me by kissing my forehead or hugging my delicate, adamant body until I softened into her touch. "There we go," she'd coo, squeezing me tighter. "It's okay to be upset, but eventually you have to let go."

In this case, I'm *not* angry about other things and projecting them onto David. I've stewed enough to determine that. I have a right to be offended by his judgment—and I don't really want an apology.

But I have to admit to myself that I want to see him again anyway. He may have hurt my feelings, but he cared how I felt. I've also never thought about a T-shirt—a man in a T-shirt—as much as I have since meeting him.

I force myself toward the last remaining boxes in the corner of my room, the ones I told myself I'd deal with before I started work. I strip back the packing tape and pull out jeans, sweaters, scarves, dumping them onto the floor. Sofia's gray sweatshirt got caught in the mix. It is the piece of clothing I asked to borrow most—oversized, pilling from being washed often, comfortable.

I think of Sofia throwing my clothes at me during our

last fight, her anger blurring rationality. I'd never seen her so furious. I'd never seen her heartbroken. "This is *yours!*" I screamed, picking the sweatshirt up from the pile in front of my feet. I shook it in her face. "You're *insane.* Who throws clothes at people in real life?" I shudder at this memory, at this other side of myself, which I secretly hoped would evaporate with maturity.

At the end of that last fight, we ran out of energy and collapsed onto separate pieces of furniture until night fell. We continued to sit in the dark, silent and spent, before Sofia retreated into the bedroom without me. The next morning, we had sex—rushed, disconnected, habitual—and didn't talk about what happened the previous day.

And here it is, the sweatshirt—our favorite piece of clothing, but ultimately *hers.* I folded it and packed it in this box, taking it with me to New York out of anger. I should have left it behind. I don't want to look at it anymore.

I place it by my door as a reminder to drop it off at the post office tomorrow morning.

III

"Lemme just say—that bitch is crazy."

My new coworker Chloe is going off about our boss, Alice, as she and I sit together at a wine bar in Manhattan to celebrate my first full week. Our knees knock against the marble surface while we drink and eat what we can before happy hour ends and the menu prices enter insurmountable territory. We've demolished two dozen oysters and two glasses of wine in forty-five minutes, just in time for more people to crowd in, unbutton their collars, and form small heaps of outerwear in the corners of the booths.

I've been waiting for Chloe's read on our manager and our office, a loft complete with wood floors, exposed pipes, brick walls, and expensive potted plants. It's all too predictable. Chloe's desk is right next to mine, but the space is almost library quiet. Talking outside of meetings is frowned upon, and headphones are assumed.

"Alice doesn't . . . smile," I say. "I know women don't have to smile but—"

"Oh please. You think I could get far in life without smiling?" Chloe flips her long braids over her bronze shoulders. She flashes me a gorgeous, toothy grin. She was out sick my first day, so I was left searching her desk to get a sense of her. When I took in the glitter gel pens, the stack of yellow notepads, the novel tucked away in the corner, and the framed photo of a cockapoo, I assumed her to be more wholesome than she seems now. "Getting through life with RBF is a *privilege*," Chloe says, tilting her head back to swallow the last few drops of her wine. A middle-aged man in a suit passes by and turns to look at her. She's oblivious, or perhaps she's used to it.

"Well, I'm glad you're here," I reply. She holds up her hand for a high five.

"Met anyone cute lately? You on the apps?" She pulls out a tube of gloss from her purse, swiping it across her lips, which already seem well glossed to me.

I've been dreading this conversation. Everyone is on the apps. I hate the idea of creating a profile. It feels fundamentally inauthentic, like bowls of plastic fruit. But I'm not sure how to date after being in a relationship for so long. Do people even meet in person anymore? I feel inexperienced even wondering.

I sigh. "I've never used a dating app. I was with my ex for five years."

"How old are you again?" Chloe asks, not quite hiding her shock.

"Twenty-five."

"Wow, that's half of your twenties." I know she isn't trying to make me feel bad, but I feel somehow plagued by my romantic history.

"Have you ever had a long-term relationship?" I ask her.

"Yes. Also for half of my twenties, but the latter half. So, I get it," she says. "But you can look forward to your thirties. Trust me." She points at herself. "Thirty-one."

"People always say that to me. That and, *You should get on the apps!*"

Chloe nods eagerly. "Well, you *should* get on the apps. Unless you're not ready. Or even better if you're not. Your first slut phase has to be wild anyway. A little reckless."

"*First* slut phase?" I try to mask the disbelief in my voice. It was not clear to me that people could have multiple slut phases. It seems indulgent. As far as I see it, either you have a lot of sex, date a bunch of people in a hobby-like fashion, or you don't. And if you don't—if you are not that person—you could partake in one single, experimental slut phase. Test the waters of your personhood.

"Well, if you choose to reenter your slut era at any point, you'll do so as a wise woman. You'll know how to enjoy yourself, but with discernment."

I'm amused by how her statement contradicts human behavior—people tend to make the same mistakes repeatedly, don't they?—but also by how much she reminds me of Jordan: bright energy, animated expressions, that optimistic way of seeing the world.

"Do you have friends here? Or is this, like, new city,

new you?" Chloe checks the clock and catches the bartender's eye.

I tell Chloe about Christian, about the party, and, because I can't help myself, about David, still enthralled by him for reasons I can't quite grasp. Chloe doesn't understand why David upset me. The more questions she asks ("Was he negging you?" "No, not exactly"; "He wasn't being derogatory, right?" "Right, but he assumed I was straight, then was *unashamedly* surprised"), the more confused I grow about my reaction. The combination of the wine and Chloe's relentless inquisition relaxes my grudge. Plus, I *was* wearing an LBD with heels to a house party, like a freshman at NYU.

I conclude my story with a dramatic reading of his message, and I wonder, out loud, if there is a chance for him to recover from offending me.

She claps her hands once, like she's settled it. "You get a ticket for Christian's show, but don't tell him," she says. "And take me along. I live for the tea."

I laugh and move my hand to my face to cover my grin. Chloe doesn't know me well, but I think she can tell she's convinced me.

"Do you think he's cute?" she asks me. I put on my best thinking face despite already knowing the answer: *Yes.* I nod at Chloe, scrunching my nose, and she squeezes my shoulders, beaming.

"What a *shock* it's going to be when he sees you," she says, wiggling her eyebrows.

We pay and practically race to the subway. Chloe

somehow manages to stand on the train without holding anything for support. She balances as if she's snowboarding. I try to mirror her, but I fall against a sweaty stranger in workout gear. "Excuse me," he says, glaring. I apologize through our stifled laughter.

My stomach hasn't stopped gurgling by the time we arrive at the venue, which, aesthetically, is a mix between a theater and a nightclub. Strobe lights glide through the darkness while a DJ presides over preshow music. I am so used to the rotation of places where my friends performed in Chicago—tightly packed venues where the audience mostly stood, small stages holding infinite talent, plastic cups of beer.

The crowd here seems more interested in getting drinks than finding a seat. But I am too distracted to do either. I inhale sharply, and my intake of breath catches Chloe's attention.

"You okay?" she asks.

"I think I might have social anxiety," I admit. "I get nervous before parties and large gatherings." *Large gatherings*, like my therapist used to say. Chloe nods empathically and says, "Go get us seats. I'll get us some water."

I choose two chairs in the back and pretend to be overly interested in my phone. I'm reading emails I've already opened when David approaches me.

"Hey, Naina." I feel the slight touch of his hand on

the nape of my neck and turn to look up. His palm rests on the back of my chair while he gazes down at me, grinning apprehensively.

"Hi, David." I give him a tight-lipped smile, unsure of how I should be responding. There is a part of me that is eager to flirt with him again, but that feels like self-betrayal based on how offended I am. Or was.

"I wasn't expecting you." He laughs. "But it's a nice surprise." He beams at me earnestly, and I feel a pang of guilt. I should be kind, magnanimous, unperturbed by our previous conversation.

"How are you?" he asks.

"I'm better after going out for drinks with my coworker today. Our boss is fond of emotional torture, I think."

"What happened?"

"Long story, but I've only had the job for a week," I say. "So, it's only going to get worse, right?"

He clicks his tongue, taking a seat. He tugs at the denim of his jeans near the knee. "As someone who's had a slew of bad bosses: Yes, it'll probably get worse. Not just them, but your tolerance level."

I shake my head.

"But hopefully I can still get the long version," he says. *I think he's flirting?* I detect the signs: the way he's leaning into me, shoulders pointing down and curving around me like a barrier, making me feel shielded and precious.

I know I don't mind it, but I'm not sure I'm ready to acknowledge I like it.

"You're a video editor, right?" I ask.

He nods. "Nothing interesting," he states. "Soulless shit. Commercials."

Chloe appears to my left, drinks in hand. I take a cup of water from her, and she offers a handshake to David. "Hi, I'm Chloe, Naina's coworker." I look at his hand, noticing a silver ring on his pointer finger I hadn't seen before. I wonder if Chloe can feel his calluses.

"David."

"Oh, I know." She flashes me a smile, and I'm horrified.

"Heard you have a mean boss," he says.

"That's one way to put it," Chloe replies.

The houselights dim. "I want to hear all about it," David whispers, his breath warm on my ear. "Your job. After the show. If you'll stick around."

"Maybe," I whisper and press my lips together to stop myself from smiling.

Christian's humor is the observational kind. He is deeply opinionated, head filled to the brim with hot takes, which, for a white man, are surprisingly uncontroversial. The root of his comedy: ridiculousness.

After the show, Chloe and I run into him outside the building, where he is being hugged by his friends. Once again, he is delighted to see me. Chloe is amused by his level of extroversion, widening her eyes at me.

"And who's this?" Christian says, wiping sweat off his forehead with the back of his hand and looking at Chloe, eyes sparkling. Chloe introduces herself, and in a matter of seconds, he invites us to join him at a bar down the block along with the rest of his crew. We start walking, about ten of us. David magically appears. I wait behind the rest of the group for him to catch up, grateful that Chloe's focus has shifted to Christian.

"What did you think?" he asks me. "Of Christian's performance."

We allow ourselves to lag behind the rest of the group. My shoulder bumps gently against his ribcage.

"He's funny," I say.

"Are you surprised?"

"No, I mean—he sees the world through a very funny lens. It's kind of compelling," I say.

David groans, incredulous. "*Christian? Compelling?*"

I stifle laughter, trying to get the explanation out. "When you think about it. Like, only *he'd* see things in that way. And it's hilarious. Oh, and *so* different from his personality. I thought he'd be cheesier."

"He's such a cheesy person." David chuckles, clearly fond of Christian and of talking about him. It's attractive to me, how much he loves his friend.

"Christian seems like he just likes to have fun," I add. "He doesn't seem too concerned with perfection. He likes to have a good time on stage. That's what matters. He's *free*. And that's what makes him so good."

"He has a gift," David says. "And he really cares about it. He nurtures it. I think a lot of talented comedians—*artists*, in general—get caught up with wanting to be 'known.'

And they stop being good because of that. Good at being themselves, I mean."

I consider that sometimes writers get too concerned with pleasing their audience before they write what's true to themselves. It's part of the reason I've been stuck recently: I have been judging my own voice by other people's standards.

David continues: "Plus, there's a level of shine to being young and successful and having clout. A lot of people give up if they don't reach that point, which is crazy to me because you have the rest of your life! And over time, I don't know . . . it's like a rat race here. Over time people forget about honing their craft. That stops being the point. The point becomes being famous."

He looks at me, checking to see if I'm still with him. I am, but I don't say anything. A moment passes between us, warm and translucent.

"Sorry, I just rambled," he says, turning away and laughing at himself.

I watch his shoulders tense, and I want to ease his discomfort. "Sorry, I was just thinking about what you were saying. I've met a lot of comedians—*people*—in Chicago who are the same way. Clout chase-y. But isn't securing fame the only way to be a successful comedian? There need to be people who show up at your shows, laugh at your jokes. Like maybe clout *is* important if you have to pay the bills. But I don't know, maybe it's a balance, like everything."

"You don't seem like a clout chaser," he observes.

"I'm not a comedian," I respond. "My best friend is, though. But I don't think he's a clout chaser."

David shakes his head. "Yeah, but you're a writer. Writers want clout, too. That's why so many of them are on Twitter."

"X."

"Okay, Elon."

I chuckle. "How'd you know I'm a writer?" I ask.

"Instagram, obviously," David responds cheekily, brushing his arm against mine. *So he looked through my profile.* He is clearly interested in me. To some extent. In some capacity.

We step into a dimly lit bar. I walk over toward Christian and Chloe, who are by the water dispenser, standing oddly close while Chloe fills a tiny paper cup. She's smiling and saying something to him while he rocks slightly from side to side, hands in pockets. David raises his eyebrows at me, and I mouth an *oh boy* back as we approach them.

Christian and David engage in mundane roommate exchanges ("Are you going to be home tomorrow? Can you sign for a delivery?"), and Chloe attempts to communicate with me telepathically. She keeps wiggling her eyebrows. It's a habit of hers, I'm learning.

"What?" I urge. "What're you trying to say?"

"Cute friends," she whispers, grinning.

"What? Them? No way. *We're* cute friends," I say, prompting a laugh from Chloe.

"David's obviously into you," she says with a self-satisfied smile. "He's not even hiding it."

"How can you tell?" I ask, failing to veil my delight at the thought of this man being attracted to me.

"How can he not be?" she says sweetly, but I want something specific. I want to hear what she sees so I can see it too.

"Please," I say dismissively.

"He knows other people here, but he chose to sit next to *you* at the show."

I wave her off, uncomfortable now that I have my answer. "What do you think of Christian?"

She shrugs. "He's giving me nerdy white boy vibes. In a cute way. Also, he's *so lean*, like a tennis player." I assume this last comment is a good thing.

"I don't think David is into me," I counter. "He just feels guilty for his weird comment and is trying to get on my good side. It probably seems like flirting because most men aren't overly concerned about leaving bad impressions."

"Impossible. Flirt with him," she suggests.

I wonder what advice Chloe would have for me if I told her the truth, so I do.

"Wanting men has never come naturally to me," I confess, somehow managing to say it coolly. "Finding them attractive, yes. Passively. But I think I feel, like, active desire right now. I've never felt that for a man before. I'm so thrown off by it. Especially since I was suspicious of him up until yesterday. And especially since that suspicion was borne of him assuming that . . . I'm attracted to men."

Chloe nods and gives me a reassuring smile. "It's okay

to be into him. It's also okay to want someone and to be thrown off by it." Not necessarily advice, but reassurance. She is kind and warm. She is nonjudgmental. I am grateful for it.

"Let's take this one." Christian turns to us, gesturing to an empty booth. A crowd pours into the bar. We sit, anticipating space will be scarce very soon.

Two hours later the music is louder, the bar darker, and our table somehow stickier. The initial group we arrived with thins out, heading off to more Friday night commitments. After a period of shouting over competing sounds—a cluster of friends clinking glasses, early 2000s indie hits with earworm choruses, and at one point, glass breaking—we're left with no choice but to whisper into each other's ears: Chloe and Christian, David and me.

He and I sit next to each other, across from Chloe and Christian. The low lights create a haze around us, making David's features seem softer and more animated. I notice the way his eyes dart around, paying attention to his surroundings, before the intensity of his gaze shifts and he focuses on me.

"When do you write?" David asks me. "Early morning? Late nights?"

"Late nights," I say. "I have trouble sleeping anyway. But I am struggling to write these days. I'm not feeling super inspired or motivated."

His breath hitches slightly. His fingers drum on his beer glass with a light, nervous rhythm. It's impossible to ignore how close he is to me now; I watch his chest rise and fall.

"Writer's block?" he asks, leaning in toward me.

I am keen to let him know I've considered solutions. "I think so. Maybe I need to find a group or something, like a writing group. At some point."

David takes a deep breath. "I have a thought."

"What's that?" I ask, hoping I don't sound as eager as I feel.

His shoulders tense, and he shifts uncomfortably in his seat, clasping his hands together to stop the jittery drumming. "Well, first I need to apologize—"

I cut him off, waving my hands. "No, no, no. Don't apologize. It's whatever—"

"I need to. Can you let me?"

"Okay, fine. It'll be more for you than for me."

He visibly steadies himself. I take in the slight flush of his cheeks, the way his eyes soften as he searches for the right words. He looks down, as if preparing, before bringing his eyes to mine. "That was very weird of me, at the party. I'm sorry for what I said. It was . . . offensive under the guise of being flirtatious. I'm sorry I made you uncomfortable. And for being presumptuous." He relaxes a bit and sips his beer. "I don't like saying the wrong thing, but sometimes I just do. Anyway, if you'll forgive me, and if we can start over, I think it would be cool to get together and write. Work on our own stuff, keep each other company, or maybe riff—whatever it is, I'd love to do it."

I am not good at responding to apologies, in part because I don't apologize much. Apologies are cards that must be dealt carefully. Like tears. I learned this at thirteen, when my mother died. I know women are primed to ask forgiveness for everything—to say "sorry" when someone runs into them—and to accept any expression of remorse with a perfunctory "no problem."

I surprise myself when I consider taking David's seriously.

"I think we've already started over, David," I say, gesturing to the bar, to how close we're sitting next to each other. He leans even more with a shrug, clearly still eager to earn my forgiveness.

The way his lips curve into a shy smile unravels something in me. I feel a strange mix of relief and anticipation. Relief because we've traversed our initial awkwardness, anticipation because we've entered entirely new territory.

"You are forgiven," I say with a nod. "For being presumptuous." He bows slightly, hands pressed together over his heart, and I laugh at him. I feel the last of my reservations melt away with this silly gesture.

"Now back to the writing conversation," I say. "I want to work on an essay about the repercussions of internet virality."

David looks confused. He rests his head on his palm attentively and absentmindedly fingers his hairline. "Say more."

"Have you heard about that guy who love bombed and then ghosted a bunch of women he met off dating apps?" I ask. I hadn't told anyone about the essay yet. It existed within the confines of my brain like a precious gem. David shakes his head and rests both of his elbows on the table, pushing his beer toward me and inching even closer, putting his ear near my mouth to hear me better.

"Okay, so two women—influencers—posted videos about their interactions with a man who was quickly affectionate and who later disappeared on them. But then, their followers—in their respective comment sections—figured out it was the same guy—"

"No!" David exclaims, smacking the table. I nod back excitedly.

"That's not even the best part, though. Once they realized it was the same guy, their stories spread even more thanks to the algorithm, and then more women shared stories of their interactions with the same man. And then other women—his 'victims' *and* people who love sleuthing on the internet—started posting photos of his face and screenshots of his text messages. Of course, it all went crazy viral. One of the funnier things that they posted was this music playlist, which he sent to basically everyone he dated, claiming it was 'specially made' for each woman. Now there's hundreds of videos out there about him. These women managed to unearth his full name and occupation." I down my beer and slosh it around in my mouth, absorbing the amused look on David's face. His left brow hitches slightly higher, signaling he is invested.

"Honestly, I can't get over how the women figured it out," he says. "That's kind of awesome. Are comment sections basically discussion boards now?"

"That's exactly it," I reply. "Comment sections are like niche community hubs. But also *what about the algorithm?* Isn't it kind of crazy that these videos just landed on the right people's pages?"

"I'm less shocked by that than the playlist thing. I mean, that's wild." David chuckles.

I feel a twinge of excitement at our shared interest in the story, almost like this conversation is our own form of foreplay. The skin around his eyes crinkles, and I study the silver peeking through his dark curls, tighter than my own.

"How old are you?" I ask him.

He laughs, surprised. "I just turned thirty-two, remember? Why? How old are you?"

"Twenty-six. Soon."

"Do you think I'm old?"

"Yes."

He squints, taking me in with a smirk.

I poke his side with my elbow. "No, you're not old. But you are *older*, so I'm not surprised you don't know much about internet culture."

"Hey, I know some things."

"I'm sure you do. I probably have something to learn from you."

"You have that new-NYC-transplant glow," he says. "So, I have something I can learn from you, too. Other than all this piping hot internet gossip."

I feel a rush of warmth, as if his attention is a tangible thing wrapping around me.

"Why'd you move here?" I ask. "Did you have dreams?"

He laughs. "Of course I did. I was an idealist."

"What did you want?"

He suddenly turns sheepish. "I wanted to write and direct my own movies. I did for a bit—shorts. A few made it into festivals, but it felt like nothing was actually happening. Then I don't know. I kind of lost that hunger, got comfortable freelancing. Now I work on my friends' projects sometimes, which is fun, but it's not the same."

"So you're not writing anything?" This lands more harshly than I intend. Embarrassment flickers across his face, and it makes me want to reach out and comfort him. My hand inches closer to his elbow on the table but not near enough to graze it.

He shrugs. "I have ideas, but I haven't written anything in years. I start but then give up. Oh, don't look at me like that—my curse won't rub off on you."

"I just feel bad."

"Don't feel bad for me."

"I don't feel bad for *you*. I feel bad that capitalism takes away our magic."

He returns to the nervous tapping. The way he flicks his now empty beer glass seems to punctuate the moment, his gestures and words blending into a shared sense of melancholy. I'm drawn to the way he reveals himself.

"I really do think we could riff off one another," he says more assertively. "I have this idea for a short . . . I don't know; it's all over the place in my head right now. But I could use some company. Some accountability. And discipline . . . all the things." He spreads his arms apart, palms face up, *what're you going to do?* and laughs.

"I think I could use all of that, too," I respond, and he gives me a satisfied, goofy thumbs-up.

"I do think the guy's playlist was kind of amazing," I blurt. "The love bomber? There was, like, Mazzy Star on there."

"I'm starting to understand his technique. Reel 'em in with sad girl music," he says, laughing.

"Yeah. Maybe I would've fallen for it, too."

I reach for my beer glass, just condensation now, to have something to do with my hands. I've always considered writing a solitary act. But now, my interest in David is coinciding with my desire to try something new, to feel more secure in my place in the world. To feel like I made the right decision moving to New York.

Sitting so close to him, warming up to each other, feels like something rigid in me is melting, going pliable.

He beams, crooked teeth and all. "Fallen for it? I bet you would have called him on his shit faster than you left my apartment."

IV

The following week, I'm standing in the middle of my room next to a pile of clothes I've deemed "unwearable."

"Wait." Jordan's face reappears on my phone screen. "Sorry, I was peeing—so wait, you're going over to this guy's *apartment*? For *dinner*?"

"Yes," I say. "And now I'm struggling to find something to wear, so please tell me if this outfit looks okay."

"Eh," he comments after a quick look. I sigh and pull the sweater over my head.

"This is such a waste of time," I whine. I tilt my phone away from Jordan to give myself some privacy. "I hate this. My brain space should be reserved for . . . other things. Not fashion."

"Who do you think you are? Steve Jobs?"

I peel off the jeans I tried on. "Fuck. What's that Margaret Atwood quote again? A man watches you . . . or something?"

"A man inside a woman," Jordan states.

"No, no. That's not it."

"You're right; that's *so off*. Especially for you, who's never had a man inside of you," Jordan teases.

"*Hey!*" I shriek, fake angry. We howl with laughter.

Once we recover, I remember the quote. "It's 'You are a woman with a man inside watching a woman. You are your own voyeur.'"

"Ah. So you think your nerves are all because of male validation?"

"Definitely," I reply. "Caring about my outfit has political undertones. I am not fully sure I can trust what I'm feeling."

"You like him, right?" Jordan asks. I "eh" him back, and he laughs.

"I don't know him," I finally say. "I'm still getting to know him. I think I'm into him, but I'm not sure why, and for some reason, I feel . . . bad about it."

"Stop intellectualizing your feelings. It won't help you," Jordan says.

I always care about what I look like, to some degree. But for me, getting ready is usually more about being presentable—patting the baby hairs down, making sure there isn't anything in my teeth, washing my face—than it is about dressing to be desired. *Is that what this is?* I try to think back to getting ready for dates with Sofia, in the early days of our relationship. Then anxiety strikes.

I tell Jordan, "Please just make sure this doesn't get to Sofia. I don't want her spinning some sort of narrative about me, off whatever this is."

"What, that you're going on dates with men? That narrative?"

"Jordan . . ."

"I won't, Naina. But cut Sofia some slack. She's not heartless. Or biphobic."

"You're right."

"I know."

"What do you think of this?" I pose, jutting out a hip, to present my outfit—a big button-down and loose, wide-leg pants absurdly accessorized with oversized hoop earrings. I've worn myself out, quite literally.

"Um, cute," Jordan replies half-heartedly. "Do you feel confident? That's what matters."

I laugh. "What?" Jordan says with a confused grin.

"I think I have a crush. That's why I feel so *off*," I admit. "Like, is it possible to *ever* be fully confident when you're into someone? Regardless of gender."

"I think the hope is that over time, you get to know someone, and you don't put them on a pedestal anymore," Jordan reasons. "And once they're off that pedestal, if you still want them, then you know it's more than a crush. *Regardless of gender.*"

I examine myself in the mirror. "I mean, there's always the black dress." I snort, and Jordan cackles.

I'm ten minutes early. David insisted I not bring anything, but I feel strange showing up empty-handed. I circle David's block twice, stopping by a bodega to grab a six-pack of beer. I buzz his apartment and travel back up those creaky steps, trying not to think too much of my last entrance and exit. He's waiting for me at the top of the stairs, his front door open, a kitchen towel draped on his left shoulder.

"So glad you're here!" he says, reaching toward me with outstretched arms.

"Thanks for having me." I hug him back and let myself consider the experience of it and of him.

He smells ridiculous, a mix of sautéed garlic and sandalwood. He's wearing a T-shirt, gray, and it seems a bit too small on him. I glance down at his feet: house shoes.

"Your apartment looks different without a hundred people inside of it," I announce. Tonight, the lights are low. Music—something I haven't heard before—plays softly from a speaker. I notice, for the first time, a small, round kitchen table. It must have been buried underneath half-empty bottles and cans. Polaroid photos cover his fridge. The last time I was here, someone's back had been pressed up against it.

I hand David the beer—"Of course you did, even though I told you not to"—and he stows it away before returning to the stove. He gestures for me to sit.

As he settles back into his cooking, adjusting knobs on the stove where a pot of pasta waits to boil and sauce gleams in a sizable pan, his watch chirps, and he glances at it. His movement around his kitchen is competent, assured.

"I hope you're hungry," he says, scanning the counter

for the kitchen towel before remembering it on his shoulder.

"I'm starving."

"How's the internet-sleuthing piece coming along?" he asks.

"It's marinating in my brain." He stirs the sauce and sets the spoon down. He leans against the counter, arms crossed, his full focus now on me. I suddenly feel very self-conscious. I liked observing him without him reciprocating.

"What?" I ask him.

"What's wrong? Why're you not writing it?"

"This is going to sound very cliché, but I don't know where to start."

He tongues the inside of his cheek. "Okay, well. For the sake of brainstorming: What about the story is interesting to you?"

"Before, it was, like, the phenomenon of love bombing and ghosting," I start, trying not to censor my thoughts as they move from my brain to my mouth. "Then it slowly became about how gossip keeps us safe and the internet as a vehicle for gossip. Then it became about what I explained the other night—what happens when someone's business goes viral, when comment sections act as juries. Deciding who's guilty and who's not guilty. And consequently—and I'm not saying this is the same thing—deciding who's a good person and who's a bad person.

"The court of public opinion, basically, but via

short-form videos," David interjects, returning to the stove. I watch his forearms as he stirs, seasons, tastes.

"Exactly. So, since we last talked, I'm thinking more about the implications of . . . I don't know, having your mistakes and flaws on blast on the internet. The lifelong impact of internet mobs on one's reputation and self-esteem. What it means to have your past define you."

"Forever defined by your flaws and your past fuckups." He nods.

"Totally. But at the same time, it's kind of evil," I add. "What he did. I don't know if the punishment fits the crime, but . . ."

David knits his eyebrows together and squints. "That's a pretty strong word. Why is it evil and not, I don't know, a symptom of low self-esteem? Of being unhealed? We all hurt people when we're not doing okay. Does that make us evil?"

"Sure." I had thought about this and had fought my impulse to be quick to judge. "Maybe he's just not doing okay. And you're right—that doesn't make him evil. But he actively took his frustrations out on women. Or, I don't know, *used* women to fill the void. That's not exactly *good*, is it?"

"No," David agrees. He salts the sauce. "It's just human."

"So you don't think humans are inherently good?" I ask.

"It's the gray area of it all." He turns to grin at me,

like there's something tender about us not being in agreement. "But your piece isn't about my personal philosophy on humanity."

"I think what he did was wrong," David continues. "But random people are self-righteously deciding what kind of person he is based on this. It could impact his future, his morale. It could perpetuate a cycle of abuse. I think that's something to consider. At least for the sake of your piece."

"I don't want this to be entirely a story about how he's the victim in all of this," I explain. "But you're right—things avalanche, because of the internet. It's mob mentality unleashed on *some dude*."

David wipes his hands on the kitchen towel before tossing it to the side. He presses his palms to the counter, fingers splayed, and I catalog the shape of his knuckles and a faint scar along his left wrist.

After a moment of quiet, I look up at him and catch his gaze on my neck. He snaps back to the conversation. "Right. He's just some dude. And likely a lonely man," he finally says. "Who can't be emotionally vulnerable. That seems sad."

"Objection, your honor," I retort, shifting my tone toward something more playful and less revealing. "Speculation. Lack of evidence. Show us proof of this emotionally invulnerable man. Show the court the proof."

David shakes his head, laughing.

"Have you ever been ghosted?" he asks, but then

scrunches his nose. "Oh, never mind. Long-term relationship—that's right."

"What about you?" I ask.

The pasta reaches a rolling boil, its starchy aroma filling the kitchen. "The best smell," he remarks.

"I love it. This is very comforting."

He rinses a bunch of parsley under the faucet before delicately plucking off the leaves one by one. He arranges them meticulously on a paper towel, drying them and preserving their shape. It seems overly precious to treat each leaf individually. I'm not sure what exactly he's making.

"I've never been ghosted, but there have definitely been times when I've lost touch with people, you know?" he muses.

I squint. "It sounds like *you* ghost people."

He chuckles. "I wasn't the best in my mid-twenties. I had a difficult time forming emotional connections with people. Except maybe Christian, I guess. I look around, at my life, and I feel like I have very few people who really know me. For a long time, that was on purpose. But recently, I'm starting to realize it's become almost habitual . . . even if I *want* to be vulnerable, it doesn't mean I will be. The desire exists, but the actual practice of it is completely different."

"I think it's great," I say. "That you're paying attention to your life. You know it could be different."

He nods. "I want to *see* people," he says. "And I want them to *see me*. I think that is life."

I don't know what I thought this evening would be—less existential, definitely—but I'm brought back to the here and now when the third roommate, Rana, enters the kitchen sporting headphones, throwing a peace sign up at David and offering a brief wave to me. Just like at the party, not a single word from the woman. Instead, she noisily bites into an apple.

"She seems shyer when she's not on Molly," I joke.

"I think she's fighting with her boyfriend," he murmurs. David takes a contemplative bite of spaghetti, chewing it thoughtfully and visibly considering it, his brows furrowing, before draining the pasta through a colander. He reserves a bit of the water, streaming it into the sauce. The pan hisses.

"I don't miss the fighting. With my ex," I say before immediately regretting bringing up Sofia. Both because I don't actually want to talk about her and because I don't want thoughts of her in the room.

"Couples need to get good at fighting," he says, his back to me. "That's my hot take. Conflict is unavoidable, but if you learn how to do it, you can solve problems more quickly."

"I've never thought of it like that."

"I heard it on a podcast. Trust me, I never would've come up with something like that on my own."

David's concentrating now: tossing the noodles in the sauce, then twirling them into perfectly whorled heaps on our plates. He dusts parmesan over them and carefully dots the parsley leaves on top, like shells on a sandcastle. When he places mine in front of me—pasta in a glistening, golden-yellow sauce, embellished in bursts of green—I can't help but marvel.

"It's beautiful."

"The sauce has saffron in it," he explains. "That's why the color."

I intend to wait for him, but I don't. I fork and twirl the pasta into my mouth. I go for a second taste immediately, reminding myself to chew and swallow.

"So good," I moan, rolling my eyes back into my head. Earthy, sweet, bright. David smiles warmly with a humble shrug, but I can tell he is proud of himself.

"It's okay," I say. "You can be proud."

"All right," he replies, throwing his hands up. "I am definitely very proud of this one."

He brushes his elbow against mine as he sits beside me, pulling his plate close.

As he takes his first bite, I work up the courage to ask him about his ex. "Tell me about the last person you dated," I blurt.

David chuckles and shakes his head, chewing. "No. You first."

I laugh nervously. "Fine. Well, her name is Sofia."

"Sofia."

"We met at the beginning of my second year in college. I had a very intense crush on her. Everyone around us knew, including her. It was so obvious. I thought she was really beautiful and powerful. She just was—is—a very confident person. She is five years older than me.

She was in grad school when we met. She asked me out, and three years later, we moved in together as soon as I graduated. By then I had this, like, feeling, I guess." I take another bite of pasta, allowing myself a moment before talking about the split.

I swallow. "I had this feeling, that we weren't right for each other. Another year after that, I wanted to break up with her, but I couldn't find the courage. Our relationship was the only thing I knew. It created a sense of certainty for me that I was afraid to lose. Until that became suffocating, too—more suffocating than feeling like I had no control over my life. Anyway, I needed an excuse to leave, so I applied for jobs out here without telling her. I got one, so we broke up. And now I'm here, and we're eating pasta." I suck a noodle into my mouth for emphasis.

"So, this is a new chapter for you," he says, returning to his plate of pasta. I realize he'd stopped eating while I was talking.

"That's what I call it, yes," I reply. "A new chapter for many things."

"You're brave," he says. "I moved here with my friends. Not by myself."

I'm moved that David could see me that way—as brave. On my worst days, the decision to leave Chicago feels more like proof of weakness than courage. More giving up than taking a risk.

"Maybe I'm just an idiot. Not brave," I respond. He squeezes his eyes and shakes his head, *no way*.

After we finish our dinner, I load the dishwasher while

David scoops pistachio ice cream into bowls for us. "Don't get freaked out," he says, drizzling olive oil over it. "I promise it tastes good." He sprinkles flaky salt on top and hands me a spoon. "Haven't we had enough olive oil tonight?" I needle because it feels more natural than what I'm thinking: *I can't believe you planned dessert.* He touches his heart, scandalized by my comment.

We transition to the couch. I put my feet on the coffee table and balance the bowl of ice cream on my thighs. He sits with his legs crossed, his shoulder leaning toward me, his knee inches away from me. I have a quiet hope that the distance between us could continue to shrink.

Keys rattle outside of the door, and Christian trudges into the living room, a gym bag slung over his shoulder. His T-shirt clings damply to his chest. "Naina!" he says. "I'll spare you a hug. I just worked out. Hey, the other night was fun. How's Chloe?"

"She's good. Really busy with work," I tell him, a little evasive. The morning after the solo show, Chloe texted me, clearly hungover and in a predicament: She liked Christian but wasn't keen on dating a comedian.

He purses his lips. "Cool," he says, clearly disappointed. "Well, I'll leave you guys to it. Good night." He plods upstairs to his bedroom.

I see David and me through Christian's eyes, and I don't know what to make of the visual. "I should get going," I say, licking my spoon. I stand up to collect my things. "Thank you again for dinner. It was delicious."

"It was a pleasure," David replies, taking our bowls to

the kitchen sink. I put my jacket on and untuck my hair from the collar.

While I tug up my zipper, he stands in front of me, rubbing his hands together, his forearms flexing. The silver ring on his right index finger catches the lamplight. He absentmindedly adjusts it, noticing my gaze. "So when should we get together again? For a writing session?"

"I'll text you, and we'll figure it out."

"Okay," he says. "It's really important we write together. It's for my own good."

"For your own good?"

"I think you're going to be a positive influence on me," he states.

"Well, what about me? What if you're a bad influence on me?"

He laughs and rubs a hand across his chest. "I don't think you're the kind of person to let that happen." I don't know how he can tell what kind of person I am or how influenceable I might be, and I wonder if he's wrong.

He offers to walk me to the bus stop, and I nod, not quite ready to be alone with myself to process my time with him. We move in silence, the cold air biting our faces. My eyes water.

"Oh my God, the wind." I wipe my eyes and avoid the temptation to make a banal comment about Chicago weather.

"How often do you cry?" he asks as we arrive at the stop. "From sadness. Not the wind."

I blow a raspberry. "I don't really cry anymore. There's no point."

He scoffs. "Naina." I am gleeful, hearing him say my name. "You think you're too good for crying?"

I recall myself at thirteen, the permanence of my mother's absence enveloping me like a dark cloud. "The saddest thing that could happen to me already did. No need to cry until the next saddest thing happens."

"Don't tempt fate," he teases. I can see him deciding whether or not to press me for more and landing on no.

"When was the last time you cried?"

He curls his bottom lip as he thinks, stuffing his hands in his jacket pockets. "Years and years ago," he finally says. "I have nothing against crying. It's just hard to find a good enough reason to cry again."

"Well, that's not too far from what I just said."

The bus rolls to a stop in front of us. "That's you," he says. We hug. Our bodies are fully, unabashedly pressed against each other. The right side of my face rests against the lower part of his chest. *You are so warm*, I want to say. A button on his jacket pushes against my cheekbone.

I pull away reluctantly, and he tells me to text him when I make it home safely.

V

Four days later, I'm on the subway, resenting Alice for bringing me close to tears. After years of concerted effort to maintain a level of detachment, life presents a bad boss. I am determined never to be one of those people who shed tears in public. There's a joke in here somewhere about being That Woman crying on the subway just after moving to New York, but I can't find it right now.

I've only been working for Alice for two weeks. Two weeks of feeling shrunken. Squashed like a bug. I didn't realize something as trivial as making a mistake at work could cause me to feel so pathetic. Worse, my music is on shuffle, so some Top 40 hit is playing as the train hurtles through a tunnel, and I can't switch to something more suitable for this devastating moment, like Bon Iver or whatever.

I respond to anger and sadness similarly. My emotional response to Alice might be displaced, I know, and I can only blame her for so much. Maybe she's my karmic punishment for refusing to cry over my breakup with Sofia or to feel too sentimental about leaving Chicago.

As if summoned via my thoughts, my phone buzzes with a notification.

Sofia: hey N, hope everything is ok with you in NY. i miss you, btw. take it or leave it. thanks for sending the sweatshirt back. take care.

I miss her too, I think. Or I miss life not feeling like a rug burn.

When I get home, Jhanaki is eating takeout at the kitchen counter, which is unusual. She routinely has dinner in her room, a habit I think is simultaneously unhygienic and endearing. The apartment is quiet, no sound of Essex accents on the TV.

"Hey," she says, scrolling on her phone. I say hello back and peel off my boots. She squints at me for a millisecond, and then her face returns to its impassive form.

I glance at my reflection in our entryway mirror. My features seem permanently pressed into an expression of despair. My baby hairs are out of control.

I smile at her. "I should order takeout. I wanted to cook today, but my boss kept me so late."

She doesn't respond. I busy myself with my coat, hanging it up in the closet. "Tomorrow I'll be up around the same time as you, by the way. Maybe before. But I won't hog the bathroom. My boss just wants me to come in an hour earlier."

I'm still tender. Saying this last sentence nearly makes me well up again. I have the urge to tell Jhanaki what happened: how Alice confronted me, the way she accused me of not caring enough about my job. I'd break down to anyone who'd listen, I realize. I press my lips together.

Jhanaki clears her throat. "No problem. So I wanted to tell you—I get that you need to charge your phone in our living room for, like, sleep hygiene reasons. But your alarm is really loud and annoying." She takes a bite of pad thai with her chopsticks. A single noodle hangs from her lips, and she slurps it into her mouth.

When I first met Jhanaki and she and I had a cordial get-to-know-each-other conversation, we discussed our pandemic-induced hobbies. Hers was crocheting. Mine was staying up late watching short-form videos. Obviously, scrolling on social media isn't a real hobby, and I started to feel moralistic about this. I was embarrassed I didn't amuse myself doing something with more social capital, like joining a supper club or trying to get abs. I mentioned to Jhanaki that I wanted to combat my social media addiction by turning my notifications off at 9 p.m. and forcing myself to read a book. The key to succeeding at this was leaving my phone outside of my bedroom.

"Oh," I say. "Does it wake you up? I mean, you get up before me—"

"Yeah, I do, but, like, you let it go on and on for a really long time," she responds, never looking away from her food. "And it's really annoying. I don't know if it takes you some time to wake up and turn it off, but could you just keep it in your room?" She picks up a piece of carrot with her chopsticks, dropping it a few times before managing to eat it.

"Well, our walls are pretty thin, so I think you'd hear it anyway," I respond irritably. *I've never even seen you crochet!* I want to say.

"Yeah, but my room is on the other side of the apartment, so it wouldn't be as loud. The living room is, like, right there. Sorry, but that alarm is so annoying."

She's being petty. I notice my blue ceramic vase is missing the bouquet I bought for myself a week ago. It was five dollars, but the flowers made me happy. Positive feelings are in high demand. My face grows hot. A bubble of anger rises through my body, expanding in my chest.

"Did you throw my flowers out?" I ask her.

"Yeah. They were dead. It looked sad."

"Don't touch my shit!" I snap. Her eyes grow wide. I storm into my room. I slam my door shut, and the tension rod holding my curtains up falls to the ground. I groan loudly, rage blurring my eyesight. I'm overcome with immediate regret.

I need to get out of the apartment. Partly because of the embarrassment from losing my temper at Jhanaki and partly because I want to see David. I miss when writing could comfort me. Not being able to rely on it as a way to process my thoughts these last weeks means my emotions are about to eat me. I message David without deliberating.

Naina: do you have plans tonight?

He texts me back almost immediately, inviting me over. On my way out of the apartment, I shoot Jhanaki an apology message.

Naina: sorry bad day at work. i'll move my phone.

I don't say "apologies for my poor emotional regulation skills."

A shirtless Christian greets me at David's apartment door. Beads of water and foamy drops of soap glisten on his neck and chest, his blond hair wet and brassy. A bruise stretches across his right side.

He laughs at the sight of me. "I thought you were the pizza delivery, so I rushed out of the shower."

"What happened to your . . ." I point to his ribcage, yellow and green, ghoulish.

"Fell off my bike," he says, shrugging. "Luckily, I didn't hit my head. I wasn't wearing a helmet. It's a bit sore, but I'll be okay. Here, come in." He lets me into the apartment and jogs back upstairs.

As I take my shoes off, David comes down the stairs to greet me. He hugs me, also smelling freshly showered, soap mingling with deodorant and a distinct hint of cologne. That sandalwood scent again, undisturbed by the presence of garlic or sweat, rising like a heat wave off his skin, dizzying me.

"Shitty day?" David says as we settle on the couch. I pull my knees to my chest and sigh.

"I can't write. I can't think. And work sucked."

"What happened?"

"My boss asked me to cover for someone but then reamed me out for making a mistake doing *their* job. It was like I pressed the wrong button and dropped a nuclear bomb. Or tripped on a wire and unplugged someone's respirator. We work in marketing, not the fucking ER." As I ramble, the anger reheats, bubbling up like lava.

"What was the mistake?" David asks.

"I linked something incorrectly in a newsletter that isn't even being sent for another few days," I respond, deadpan.

"How could you?" David shakes his head.

"How is she like this?" I mumble.

"You know"—he takes a breath—"she might have had horrible bosses. And instead of wanting to be different, she thinks she needs to pay it forward. I mean, she's probably doing that thing a lot of people in higher-up positions do, right? Put other people through the same shit they went through? Everyone's had a shitty boss—abusive, micromanaging types, whatever—and some people are more interested in having their turn than changing things." David curls his lip to emphasize his point, still shaking his head.

These are the moments when it's obvious David is older than me. He functions with a certain kind of patience and acceptance. He never seems bothered that I see things differently or that I'm harder on people, less willing to let things go.

"What should I do?" I ask. I'm surprised by how genuinely I want to know what he'll say.

He shrugs. "You could try talking to her. But she seems a bit unreasonable . . ."

"I think she invented gaslighting."

"*Men* invented gaslighting."

"Well, that makes up for everything else you've ever said," I respond sarcastically.

"Good, that's why I said it," he says, teasingly tapping my elbow. His finger lingers. My shoulders loosen, slackening from his touch. My anger drifts like a balloon, eventually disappearing.

"Thank you for listening to me vent." I take a deep breath. I was vulnerable, and nothing fell apart as a result.

"No need to thank me. I'm sure you'll hear me rant about some work thing eventually," he replies.

"I already have. Snooze fest," I say, pretending to yawn.

David playfully rolls his eyes. "Glad this friendship goes both ways."

A lump forms in my throat hearing him refer to us as friends. I conceal my disappointment with a laugh.

Did I imagine the chemistry we had that night at the bar? The tension between us the other night at dinner? *He'd cooked for me.* I guess friends make pasta for each other. I guess they drizzle olive oil over ice cream and walk each other to bus stops.

Do I want male validation so badly that I'm imagining there's something between us?

"To be honest," David says, tapping my elbow again, this time with his knuckles, "you're a really good listener."

"Really?" I ask. He nods. I squeeze his forearm, and he responds with a smile, as if he was waiting for me to touch him.

Was he?

"Thank you. I try. And speaking of which—you never told me about your short film idea," I remind him. "Have you been working on it? Are you going to work on it now?"

He nods and pulls his laptop off the coffee table. "I wrote an outline."

He hands his computer to me, and I read the setup, about a man who brings a date back to his apartment. At first, it seems like the story is about the man. But the moment they're in his bedroom, obviously about to have sex, different versions of the man—him as a child, then as a teenager, then as a twenty-something—appear before the woman.

"The point is that we get caught up in narratives about what 'men and women are like'"—he adds dramatic air quotes. "Think Tall Curly Haired Guy and Beautiful Girl Who Works in Marketing." I punch his arm, and he puts his hand on my thigh, keen to explain himself. I am delighted to be touched by him; it sends shock waves through my system, and I am suddenly still, clinging to every word he says. *Beautiful.*

He continues: "No, but really. We end up treating people as archetypes rather than as people. So, this woman's assumptions about the man are challenged by these younger versions of him. And in the same way, she challenges the assumptions other people have created about her." He lifts his hand off my thigh, and I immediately miss it.

"What happens at the end?" I ask.

"I'm not sure. This is the first time I feel like I have something to say. Historically, I just wrote and shot what I thought would be cool or funny. I hope this will be cool and funny too, obviously."

"So when are you going to start writing it?"

He shrugs. "I think now. If you were serious about a writing session."

"I very much was."

"Okay, but want some tea first?"

It's late, and even if I leave now, I won't get more than four hours of sleep. David and I have been talking, nonstop, after a long stretch of typing punctuated by short distractions ("Did you know a pickup artist invented negging? A guy named Neil Strauss"; "Sorry to disturb your flow, but

I really think we should get some snacks"). We finished writing an hour ago, and he's slumped into an armchair, legs outstretched on the ottoman while I sit cross-legged on his couch.

"I need to go home," I finally say.

He checks his watch, which, I realize through our silent working time, beeps at every hour. "It is 2 a.m.," he agrees.

We sit in silence for a moment. I don't feel like leaving.

"I feel awful. I was so rude to my roommate tonight," I confess. "I went home in a horrible mood after work, you know, and she had a simple request. For some reason, it pissed me off. I snapped at her."

"What was the request?"

"To keep my phone in my bedroom at night. So the alarm doesn't bother her in the mornings. Apparently, I sleep through it for a long time before I wake up."

"Heavy sleeper, huh?"

"Yes. My girlfriend—ex-girlfriend—would have to shake me awake. Meanwhile, I'd be dreaming I was on a boat in a storm or something."

"Do you get nightmares?"

I tell him the truth, something I've only ever shared with my last therapist. "I do. They can be really disturbing, and sometimes I wake up and feel like my entire day is ruined. I mostly dream about my mother in the hospital. Sometimes I'm screaming for a doctor because I'm afraid they've abandoned her and that she'll die from their negligence. Or my mother is talking to me but then walks away when there's something I really need to tell her. I chase after her but can never catch up." I'm not ready to tell him about my mom dying outright, but this is a start.

He nods, his hands clasped together and pressed against his mouth. He's looking up at me, wordlessly, from under those knitted, dark eyebrows. David makes it easy, I realize, to be honest. High risk is high reward with him. He is good at making me feel like I matter—and that perhaps the risk isn't as high as I thought.

"I used to get nightmares a lot," he finally says. "Then I did this thing called EMDR therapy."

"For PTSD?"

"Yes." He stands up suddenly, and I wonder if my question went too far.

"Sorry, didn't mean to push," I say.

He's in the kitchen, pouring us water. He furrows his brows. "What? No, you didn't at all—I'm just thirsty," he says. He stretches, back arched and arms raised to the ceiling. I catch a glimpse of his stomach—hairy and solid—and turn away. He brings me my glass, and I drink the whole thing in a few gulps.

"I have to be at work an hour earlier than usual," I say with a sigh. I feel a bit shy, like I overstayed my welcome, and a bit raw too: I came to David's not only to write but also, admittedly, to seek comfort. Now I feel foggy, like I'm hungover.

I find my jacket draped on the back of the bulbous couch and slip it on—denim with sherpa lining, gifted by Sofia for one of my birthdays—and tuck my head into my hat.

"I'm glad you came by. Thanks for motivating me to write," he beams.

"Any time," I respond, remembering the "friend" comment. Lemon juice on a paper cut.

"How're you getting home?"

"The bus."

David winces. "It's too late for that. Want me to drive you?"

"You have a car?"

"Christian does."

I realize if I resist, David will only insist. And he has a point: It's late.

"If I tuck my hair into my beanie, maybe no one will bother me."

He rolls his eyes. "Let me go knock on his door for his keys."

"I can just get a car," I respond with a shrug, waving my phone. "That's actually a better idea."

"You don't want me to drive you? Or do you just feel bad about me driving you?"

"The latter. So technically the former, too."

David gives me a stern look. "One sec." He walks upstairs, and I hear him knock on Christian's door. After a quick, muffled exchange, he jogs back downstairs, holding the keys up to me.

"I can drive you. But I don't want to push if you're

uncomfortable. I just need you to know you're not an inconvenience."

I don't worry about being an inconvenience to David, for some reason. His generosity lands so sweetly that I am willing to say yes, even if only to spend more time with him.

When we climb into Christian's Chevy Malibu—"Terrible choice. Seriously, he's going to have issues with it soon. His parents know nothing about cars"—David adjusts the mirrors. His driving is steady and focused. His hands remain firmly at ten and two, his posture upright and alert. I've never seen someone sit so uncomfortably in the driver's seat. He looks like he hates being there, but he's doing it all the same.

"This song," he says, turning up the music. He hums.

"What is it?"

"It's the *algaita*. It's a West African wind instrument. No sad girl music tonight, just vibes," he says, grinning.

"Where are you from?" I ask him. "Why haven't we talked about this?"

He shrugs. "Why talk about it? Don't people come here to escape where they're from?"

"Don't be corny. You know I'm from Chicago and that my parents are Indian. What about you?"

"Thanks for not asking me what kind of brown I am this time. I'm from Delaware. I'm Persian."

"I figured. From your last name."

"You knew I was from Delaware because of my last name?"

I swat at him. "Dad joke."

He snickers, eyebrows raised mischievously.

He pulls up to my apartment building. He yawns, then I yawn, our eyes glittering.

"Thank you," I say, unbuckling my seat belt.

"Hang in there at work tomorrow." He squeezes my shoulder. I move to hug him, and I lean in so abruptly that he's caught by surprise. His arms brace around my shoulders, as if to steady me, then quickly soften, as if giving my body guardrails.

"You're cool," he says when I pull away. "I like you."

David is my friend, despite his dizzying smell. David is my friend, even if I've had to tear my eyes away from his arms. My friend with kind smiles and soft features and good advice that doesn't even annoy me. Who doesn't hide how he feels, who values this, our friendship.

I grin and respond, "I like you too." My heart races with uncertainty, unsure if my words convey the depth of my affection or just a deep fondness for our newfound camaraderie. David's watch beeps, and he looks at the time.

"We should get some sleep."

He doesn't drive away until I'm inside. After I wash my face and change my clothes, I collapse into bed. The next morning, I wake up and check my phone. He texted me shortly after dropping me off.

David: You left your bag with your laptop here. Not your work laptop, I hope? I can bring it to you tomorrow. Let me know.

VI

I stumble down the subway steps to catch the train to work, but it is already speeding away from me by the time I make it through the turnstile. With five minutes to spare until the next one, I type out a message to Sofia.

Naina: hey, glad you got the sweatshirt. hope all is well.

I consider saying more, but I want to be measured.

Sofia and I met when I was a sophomore in college, and she was a graduate assistant. At our Gender and Sexuality Resource Center on campus, I often spent time studying and lounging on the dusty university furniture with other undergrads. I felt safe amongst other queer people—free to be myself, no questions asked—but I also needed the validation. I felt gawky about my queerness, so internally gay but never sure if it translated externally.

I think Sofia sensed I needed to be brought out of my shell. I'm still grateful for it, and I probably always will be. We had a lengthy honeymoon phase for a year and a half, most of which was just hooking up and going on romantic dates without a label for our relationship. It seemed like everyone knew about us—our friends, the students who spent time at the center, even some professors who'd seen us holding hands in the early morning, walking from her residence hall to the café.

She had a shag haircut back then, dyed jet black, and her sharp blue eyes sparkled beneath her bangs. Before we ever talked, I snuck glances at her body: long and lean, her chest flat. I've always been envious of women with small tits; I constantly felt like I was wrangling my boobs into clothes before I fully embraced proper bras. She wore European League football jerseys or linen button-downs. In the winter, she tucked herself into sweatshirts layered over turtlenecks. I never saw her in skinny jeans or anything formfitting. When we got together, I relished taking off her baggy clothes, having her on top of me, running my hands down her tight waist.

She never formally asked me to be her girlfriend. Being in a committed relationship with her felt like the inevitable outcome, especially when she told me she wasn't seeing other people. We only started having problems when we moved in together, three years into dating. Our lives had become enmeshed, and at first, that felt like a pure, unconditional love sort of thing. But our lack of boundaries triggered the worst in us: my tenacity, other-wise known as grudge holding, and her pessimism, which often arrived in the form of criticism.

It hurt to no longer have access to her—her life, her

thoughts, her friends. Plus, the idea of Sofia out there having sex with someone other than me burned. But experiencing these emotions felt unfair, especially when I was the one to end things. She deserved to be happy, and ultimately, I wanted her to move on.

I reread my message, a nothing response to hers. I hit send.

"David is definitely into you," Jordan says to me over the phone. "Don't be naive."

"I'm not being naive," I insist, louder than intended. A man walking past me on the sidewalk flashes a curious stare before disappearing forever.

I'm walking back to work from grabbing lunch, starving after arriving early as promised. A motorcycle roars past, and I plug one of my ears, screaming into the phone. "I just feel like we have more of a friend vibe right now. Which is what I need, I guess. And like I told him, I'm not into men."

"No offense, but you've known him for, what? Over three weeks now? And he's going out of his way to give you a ride at two in the morning? When you could take a car? Either he's into you or he's friend love bombing you."

"*Friend* love bombing?"

"It's a thing. That's what I did to you."

I laugh. "That's different! Friendship is different!"

"It's a relationship," Jordan says. "And a bomb is a

bomb. Here's my question. How into him are you, exactly? What is your level of attraction?"

I think about David's scent for what feels like the millionth time. It's like I can still smell him if I try hard enough. I think about his silver ring, sort of improperly fitted, squeezing around his thick finger. Him tearing parsley leaves off the stem, holding his breath. The veins snaking up his forearms. The way he crosses his legs when he's listening hard or stretching them out onto anything—the coffee table, the ottoman—when he's relaxed. His cautious way of driving.

"I know this sounds crazy, but when I think about him, I don't think about the way he looks. I mean, that's not the first thing that comes to mind."

"What do you think about, then?"

"The way he asks questions, or how intense he gets when he's sharing his opinions." I step off the curb and smile to myself. "And he smells really good."

Jordan laughs. "Pheromones, baby. Your body is telling on you."

David and I make plans to meet at a random comedy show.

When I ask Chloe if she wants to come along, she sighs.

"Do you know if Christian will be there?"

I shake my head.

"He and I went on a sort of date recently, and it was honestly amazing, so good. But then I didn't text him back, so now I feel bad, but I also am avoiding him."

I laugh and shake my head. "You're playing games, Chloe."

Without the buffer of a plus-one, I worry about the tone of this meetup—that it will feel like a date. That I might want it to.

When I get to the venue, concealed in the basement of a three-story building, I recognize a few people from the party in the audience, squeezed into rows of four. I catch sight of Margot, who flashes me a smile. I wonder if she would be as warm if she saw me with David.

I wait for him at a small table at the back of the audience, nervous I chose too intimate a seating arrangement. He finds me, and when he leans down over me, I feel awkward about the way our arms try to arrange themselves into a hug and how my body responds to this amicable form of contact.

"I just saw Rana's ex," he whispers as he sits down, conspiratorially pulling his chair close. "They *just* broke up."

"Oh wow. Were you friends, you and her ex?"

"Sort of," he says. "But honestly? I'm glad they broke up. She seems relieved. She's also deeply avoidant. Took forever for her to even get together with him. Not that I'm one to talk."

His last sentence, although offhanded, makes my chest clench. I note my discomfort, and the word *detach* echoes in my mind, like some sort of protective spell I'm casting over our friendship. I would hate to be on the other end of what I assume to be David's self-proclaimed avoidant tendencies.

After the show, I exchange another glance with Margot, who doesn't smile this time.

David and I could have easily parted ways, since he brought my laptop with him, but instead, we're taking the subway back to my place. I don't know who initiated, just that neither of us resisted.

His various subway stances are comically masculine. Sometimes he stands with his arms crossed, hands tucked under his armpits, balancing despite the train's lurches. Other times he extends his arm over his head, hand white-knuckling the subway bar. My neck hurts from looking up at him. I am nearly pressed up against him, thanks to the late-night crowd packed into the train car. The smell of him radiates off his armpit, deliciously human.

"My boss, Alice, said she finds improv cringey," I tell him. He rolls his eyes.

"She's clearly never had a cringe phase."

I shrug. He goes on: "To become a 'cool person,' you need to be okay being weird and sharing those weird parts of yourself with other people. Your boss is hating because she's uncool."

"She's definitely uncool."

The train pulls to a stop, and I lose my balance. He steadies me by gripping my right bicep.

"Naina, just hold the pole. What're you trying to prove? Anyway," he continues, "everyone has to figure themselves out, you know, what kind of person they are in this world. But to do that, we have to embarrass ourselves over and over again. Take risks. Find out what we like and don't like. That's the journey to coolness. Cool people rarely cringe. Because they know what it's like to be cringe."

I wonder about David's relationship to his past versions of himself, what he deems as *uncool* in retrospect.

When we get to my place, I'm relieved Jhanaki is in her bedroom. She accepted my apology, but since then, our conversations have been stilted.

David hasn't been to my apartment before, and he seems nervous. He sits on my couch, and his chattiness comes to an abrupt halt.

I busy myself unwrapping the deli sandwiches we picked up along the way and break the silence with the question I've been thinking all evening. "Is it weird to see your ex? Margot?"

Surprise sweeps across his face, but he quickly conceals it. "Not anymore. It used to be."

"What's the story there?"

He shrugs. "We dated for a couple of years. It didn't work out."

"How long ago?"

"Like two years ago?"

"Why didn't it work out?"

"Just not compatible." There is an evasiveness in his tone that feels strangely out of character.

"Right. Well, *my* ex texted me yesterday," I say, hoping my honesty will make him feel safe enough to share more.

"Really? What did she say?" He shifts his body on the couch, settling in.

"I mailed back a sweatshirt of hers. She thanked me and told me she missed me."

"What did you say?"

"That I hope she's doing well."

"Cold."

"Not trying to be."

"You don't miss her?"

A wave of emotion rushes over me. I remember how it felt to put my head on her lap, have her rub my scalp. Her bony back facing me in the mornings, the warmth of her pressed against me under the covers.

Anger arrives quickly, unforeseen in this private moment of nostalgia. In hopes of getting somewhere deeper with David, I exhale and tell him the truth: "I stayed in the relationship for too long out of fear. I felt resentment toward her, but I was scared to let her go. I seethed in my own anger, a lot. Then I started to resent *myself*."

I take in David's expression. I didn't scare him off. He is looking at me in earnest; he is here with me in this moment, head cocked to the side, taking in every word I am saying.

"To answer your question, I do miss her," I add. "But maybe it's just the familiarity."

"I get that," he says. "Resenting yourself for being complacent. I think a lot of people struggle with that. I know I do." David, revealing his imperfections, only makes me fonder of him.

"Well, good thing you don't live in Chicago," he continues. "Familiarity keeps you trapped."

"What does that mean?"

He rubs his eyes with his free hand and yawns. "I mean exes hooking up after the breakup. Makes it a lot harder to move on."

"Says who?"

He shrugs at me. Takes a bite. I watch his jaw as he chews, his throat as he swallows.

"Give me an example," I insist. "Of the incompatibility."

He looks at the ceiling, blinking slowly. He has a smear of mustard on his upper lip, and I don't know what to do about it. "Uh . . . well, I don't get very jealous. But she was a pretty jealous person. I mean—we'd run into someone I dated or hooked up with in the past. Then there would be a lot of anger. It would build up, then explode, then we'd fight."

Building up, exploding, fighting—this is all familiar to me, but not on the receiving end.

"Are you saying she was insecure?"

He teeters his head, *comme ci, comme ça*. "Sure, but I think people are allowed to get jealous. She wasn't communicative. I also think I was fed up and couldn't be . . . consolatory."

"Ah, I can see it. *Babe, it was just one time. Chill out!*" I lower my voice to imitate him, and he laughs one of his big laughs.

"That's what I sound like?"

"I'm not an impressionist."

"What about you?" he asks, crossing his legs. "How were you and Sofia incompatible? Or compatible?" He takes another bite of his sandwich and leans back into the couch.

I sigh. "I think we were compatible because she guided me out of being a baby gay. Okay, no, I'm not giving us enough credit. She was excellent at taking care of me, emotionally and physically. But she could also be very controlling and judgmental."

I choose to omit my emotional outbursts. The word *codependent* rings in my head, but I don't want to share that, either. I'm still working on owning up to my flaws.

He nods. "She was older than you, right?"

"By five years."

"What do you think she saw in you?"

I wince, remembering. "I mean, I stared at her all the time. I fantasized about her. I definitely put the moves on her first."

"Okay. But then what was it about *you*?"

"I think she saw that I admired her. And was willing to love her. Can't that be enough?"

"Maybe you're not giving yourself enough credit, or her. I feel like there's plenty of other things you could say."

"Like what?"

He wipes his mouth with a napkin, and the mustard disappears. "I dunno. I mean, obviously we didn't know each other back then, but I'm sure you were just as clever and ambitious. Hardworking. Intuitive. Great comedic timing."

I twist my face to prevent a grin. He laughs. "It's okay. Take the compliment. I'm only being truthful."

Desire tugs at me. *Do I want him? Or do I want his validation? Or is it both?*

"Thank you." I press my palms together and bow.

"You're welcome."

"So who are these other people, then?" I divert. "That Margot is jealous of?"

He sighs. "Just some women I dated casually. We were never serious."

I'm both slightly annoyed and intrigued. So, David isn't completely open. He has things he doesn't want to talk about, too.

I push. "They're not exes of yours? Just women you dated?"

He shrugs. "Hooked up with."

"No other exes?"

"Not in New York, no. My last girlfriend before Margot was in high school."

"That's a long time to be single."

"Yeah, but I was never *actively* single. You know? There's a difference between hooking up with people, being noncommittal, and not participating in sex and romance at all. I've never really done the latter. Until this past year."

I realize that though David is unguarded with his observations and opinions, he isn't keen on explaining the events that brought him so much clarity and conviction.

"What about this high school girlfriend, then? Do you ever think about her? Is she the *one that got away*?" I prod.

He looks wistful for a moment—younger, boyish— and nods. "I do think about her. But she's no longer with us?"

It takes me a moment to grasp what he's saying, mostly because he said it like a question. Then, I understand. Presenting the truth as a question makes the words feel less heavy, the grief less real.

"I'm so sorry."

"It's all right. It's been years now. Obviously, stuff like that never leaves you, but I've picked up some coping skills."

"My mom died," I blurt. He raises his eyebrows. "Sorry, not trying to take away from your—I get it, is all. When did it happen?"

"Our senior year. We were together throughout all of high school. She was in a car accident."

I think about his cautious driving. His alertness at the wheel, bordering on hypervigilance. The EMDR therapy.

"Fuck. I'm so, so sorry."

"What about your mom?"

"She was ill. I was thirteen." I leave it at that.

"That's why the nightmares," he says, recalling what I told him before.

"I can't imagine losing a girlfriend," I detract.

"I can't imagine losing a parent." He reaches for my fingers, draped over my knee, and holds them for a few moments like we're completing a circuit.

We turn back to our sandwiches, allowing the surge of emotion to subside. As I clean up the wrappers and mayo packets, I ask him what he's been watching lately, now accustomed to talking about television as a fallback thanks to Jhanaki.

I flop back onto the couch and close my eyes, tired from the day.

"Do you want to sleep here?" I ask David.

He stares at me blankly. I'm not sure what to make of the expression on his face. I decide to rush through what I want to say, unveiling a desire for this night to turn out differently than the others.

"We can share my bed. Unless you want the couch. It's not that comfy, though. You don't need to go, is all I'm saying. I actually have a lot of spare toothbrushes. The free ones from the dentist."

He looks at his hands pensively.

"It's not a big deal to me," I ramble. "Unless it is to you, which in that case, I'm sorry if I'm making you uncomfortable."

David bursts into laughter. "Yeah, yeah, I feel very violated right now." He sighs and runs his hands through his hair, blinking at the space in front of him. "Sure, why not? We can get coffee in the morning, and I'll give you a pep talk before work."

My body surges with satisfaction. Everything around me has evaporated, and I realize I'm experiencing pure thrill, which I haven't felt in a very long time.

David brushes his teeth while I struggle to find something to wear. *You're literally getting dressed for sleep, dumbass*, I tell myself. But a little tank is too suggestive, and a full set of pajamas seems excessive. I'm still figuring it out when David enters my bedroom.

"What's up?" he says.

"Going to change," I reply.

"I give off a lot of body heat," he warns. "If that influences your sleepwear."

I blush, unsure if he's somehow aware of my current dilemma. I shake my nerves off. "Good to know," I respond, settling on an oversized Wieners Circle T-shirt.

I change in the bathroom. Scrubbing my face, I find myself unrecognizable in the mirror. I am jittery but also renewed: I admitted to wanting something, and I asked for it—or rather, offered it. This is the opposite of running away. I feel like I am sprinting toward something, full force.

When I reenter my room, David is sitting on the edge of my bed. He asks me which side I sleep on. He won't look me in the eye. I point to the right, where the bed meets the wall. He yawns, and his watch beeps. "I can't believe it's already two in the morning." He shakes his head.

He's still on his phone when I crawl under the covers. I tell him to use my charger.

"I sleep in my underwear," he says hoarsely, standing to plug his phone in. "Is that—"

"I figured," I say.

"And without a shirt. But I don't have to."

"I think I'd prefer that." He smirks in response.

"More than with your outside clothes in my bed," I say.

"Right."

He takes off his pants, the metal on his buckle clinking. I busy myself scrolling, but I'm not even looking at what's on the screen. I'm sneaking periphery glimpses like a creep. I've never shared a bed with a man except for Jordan, I realize.

David's forearms flex as he folds his shirt—*folds it*—and places it on my chair with his pants. He's wearing boxer briefs. His chest is hairy. As he slips into my sheets, I pass him my phone to put on the nightstand. He takes his watch off.

"You can turn off the light," I say, gesturing to the lamp. He flips the switch, and we're in complete darkness, lying next to each other, shoulders touching.

"Thanks for letting me crash here," he says.

"It's no big deal," I repeat. But it is a big deal. I know it is, because I can feel it in my body.

I've somehow forgotten how to breathe. Now inhaling and exhaling feels like a performance. I decide to count to one hundred, and when I get to sixty-something, I soften, and the idea of another body next to mine comforts me. Of David's body.

I turn my back toward him and curl up on my side. After a few moments, I feel a weight on my back, and I wonder if David has placed his hand there.

I know it's only my imagination when David's arm—his actual, real-life arm—loops around me, over my chest.

"Is this okay?" he asks, whispering, and a surge of electricity travels up my spine.

"Yes," I reply.

"Okay, good."

I feel his breath on the back of my neck, rhythmic and steady, turning the spark that surged through me moments before into something more liquid. I press my back into him, and he responds with a low, satisfied hum. We fall asleep like that and wake up like that too.

VII

The third time David sleeps over, he meets Jhanaki for the first time. While she fries her eggs and I wait for the coffee to percolate, the two of them launch into a passionate discussion about television. They are coming to a consensus on a list of "uncancelable" shows, veering off into a tangential breakdown of scenes from *Flames Flicker Eternal*. Jhanaki deems the "teens doing drugs and having sex" show irredeemable.

"What!" David says. "But it's shot so well. And honestly, some of the characters are really lovable. Like that one girl who dresses up as Bob Ross for Halloween."

"That's not a bad idea actually," I say, wiggling my eyebrows, something I picked up from spending most of my days with Chloe.

"I dare you," David teases.

Right after he slips out of the apartment, Jhanaki whips around to me. "Are you guys a thing?"

I shake my head. "We don't have sex. It's just cuddling."

"Really? How long have you guys been hanging out?" I can see her wheels turning. Jhanaki catches herself, attempting to reel her curiosity back in. "I mean, I know it's none of my business—"

"We're not hooking up. Really. We've had—sleepovers, I guess? A few times. For two weeks." Jhanaki's eyes grow wide, and I attempt to quell her shock: "We just feel . . . very safe with each other. I like him. But I haven't told him yet."

She plates her eggs and drizzles hot sauce on top, shaking the bottle aggressively to get the liquid out. "I've seen this play out before," she says before stabbing the yolk with a fork and taking a generous bite. "You guys have a friends-to-lovers thing going on."

"I'm not sure if what I feel is a crush," I admit. It's nice to be talking about David with her. She is a more reliable third party than Jordan, whose thirst for drama and intrigue sometimes colors his advice despite his best intentions.

"What do you mean?" Jhanaki asks.

"Do you know what compulsory heterosexuality is?"

She scoffs. "Of course I do. I'm gay, and I had three boyfriends in high school. What—you think you don't have real feelings?"

"Yeah. I'm not sure if I just want his validation."

"You can be attracted to a man and have sex with a man and still be gay," she points out. "It's up to you, dude. Who you want to be, what you want to identify as."

"I don't think it's a good look for me. To go from dating a woman for so long and then . . . what would my friends think? What would my ex think?"

"Your friends?"

"Yeah, like my friends in Chicago." I am mostly referencing Sofia and her gossipy, judgmental group, who'd have a field day if they knew I was dating a man.

Of course, David and I were not dating, but that is beside the point.

"Who the fuck cares? They live in Chicago. You gotta chill out. Stop questioning your queerness. It's insulting. I mean, look—*I get it*—but I also think you need to loosen up. If you like him, you like him."

I contemplate loosening up while I transform into Bob Ross. It's Halloween—or rather, it is the 26th of October, the Saturday before Halloween.

I tuck my hair into a wig cap and think about what Jhanaki said—*who the fuck cares?*—but I feel defeated. *I care.* Having a crush on David is sending me into a full-blown identity crisis. That, layered over how disoriented I feel postbreakup and only two months in New York. Discomfort has taken over my body, like an uninvited guest settling into my bones. I'm experiencing a kind of self-loathing only the middle school version of me could rival. *Am I being too hard on myself? Or not being hard enough on myself? Am I putting too much weight on my emotions toward David or not enough?*

I don't think of myself as a chaotic person. I value stability, which means maintaining some level of power over my life and the decisions I make. I do what I can to ease uncertainty. When my mother died, I realized practicality was my tool against the lack of control I felt from being alive. When my relationship with Sofia arrived at an irreparable point, the most pragmatic next steps were obvious, if difficult to execute: End things, make a change, exit my comfort zone as it became my discomfort zone. Being with her was sensible until it wasn't.

I ride my bike to Williamsburg decked out: stick-on beard, blue button-down, dad jeans, and, of course, curly wig. It is strangely warm for a fall evening. The wind ruffles my fake hair as I pedal down Union Avenue. A handful of strangers wave and call out to me while I'm waiting at a red light, validating my costume choice.

I considered dressing up as Megan Fox in *Jennifer's Body*, which Sofia would've labeled a *hot* costume. "You're not a hot costume kind of girl," she said to me a couple of Halloweens ago. That year, we went dressed as characters from a children's movie, despite my internal resistance to being stuck in a green sphere for the entire night. It was as unwieldy and sweaty as I feared.

I'm meeting David at a party. As I lock up my bike, I regret not being more insistent with Chloe after she declined the invitation to join me.

"I can't see Christian," she said. "We went to the movies yesterday and almost hooked up after. Honestly, I'm relieved I had some self-control."

"What do you mean you almost hooked up?" I asked.

"There was a vibe," she said simply, providing no clarity.

When I asked Jhanaki if she'd want to join, she just laughed.

I've been repeating the same sentence in my head since David and I started having postwriting sleepovers. *No big deal!* It is no big deal that we fall asleep spooning, no big deal that I wake up with my face buried in his chest. It is no big deal that I started thinking about David beyond his smell, beyond the way he laughs and how he interacts with his friends, all jovial and witty. I downplay the truth whenever Jordan asks about us. I haven't even told him about the overnights.

Arriving without a friend leaves me feeling unguarded, like I've arrived too eager, too willing. It is as if my aloneness speaks on my behalf: *I am here, at this party, for you. Dressed as Bob Ross.* It feels obvious now, how much I want to see David. I hate that it's written all over me, the thing I've been trying so hard to bury.

I slip into the apartment building, right as all three Powerpuff Girls leave for a smoke. Bubbles holds the door open for me. I take the elevator up a few flights even though the party is on the first floor, steadying my nerves as it hums, and I take the stairs back down.

It occurs to me that it is easier to walk into a party alone when you are in costume. I go straight to the kitchen to find a drink. I'm gulping wine and feigning interest in the fridge magnets when Christian and I spot each other.

"Naina!" he says, opening his arms wide. "I didn't recognize you!"

He is dressed completely in red: pants, shoes, shirt.

"What's your costume?" I ask as politely as possible, completely lost.

"A walking red flag," he says.

I cackle.

"Which I'm *not*, obviously," he says, laughing with me. "That's why it's a costume."

"Totally."

"Bob Ross?!"

"Indeed," I say, holding up a palette I brought along as a prop. "We don't laugh because we feel good. We feel good because we *laugh*."

"Cheers to that," he says, tapping his cup against mine. I drain my drink.

"Whoa," he says. "Slow down."

"I will after this." I had a single pollo empanada for dinner, and the wine hits me almost immediately.

"How's the bruise?" I ask him.

"It's gone. It's almost like it never happened."

"Good. But you should probably start wearing a helmet."

"Sure, sure. Wanna dance?" he asks as I pour myself another full cup, emptying the bottle.

"Let's go."

We spill into the living room and let the music swallow us whole, just the two of us. We bounce and sway together, the wine transforming my jittery nerves into a heady, intoxicating euphoria. A few others drift toward the music like moths. I close my eyes, letting the beat take over, my head bobbing so hard my wig slips, despite the copious amount of glue I'd used earlier. A hand reaches out, tugging it back into place. I turn to see a woman in a Ghostbuster costume. She's smiling at me, and it takes a second before I realize—it's Margot. David's ex.

"Margot!" I say excitedly, pulling her into a tipsy embrace. She hugs me back, and we continue to dance. Eventually, the group breaks apart, and Christian and I are left alone again.

"Where's David?" I shout over the speakers.

"Dunno. Let's go find him!"

We venture out into the backyard, which is crammed with people mingling under the glow of string lights, a collage of characters. Christian lights a cigarette.

"Want one?" he asks.

"Why not." He lights it for me, and I'm immediately dizzy from the first drag. I smoke it anyway.

"What's going on with you and Chloe?" I ask. He shrugs with a sigh.

"Not sure. Sometimes I think she's into me. But then she stops texting me, and I can't tell if I'm being annoying or something. I think she's really cute." He exhales a cloud of smoke. "Is this weird? For you?"

I wave my hand. "It's whatever."

"Does she talk about me?"

"No," I respond quickly, lying, and Christian's face falls. I backpedal, taking the cigarette from him. "But I know she thinks you're cute, too."

He masks a satisfied grin with a drag and an exhale.

"I see him. David!" Christian calls out for him while

the wine and nicotine rush to my head. I don't turn around, choosing to ash my cigarette instead.

As Christian pulls David, dressed as Inspector Gadget, into a hug, I realize he isn't alone. A majestic woman dressed as Lara Croft is smiling at Christian. She's wearing a tank top and tiny shorts, revealing remarkably long and spray-tanned legs. Christian calls her Natasha and embraces her warmly. David and I lock eyes. It takes him longer than I'd like for him to realize it's me underneath the costume.

"Oh my God, Naina. *You didn't.*"

I laugh weakly and shrug as David gives me a one-arm hug. I feel small, and it's not just because I'm standing next to two gorgeous giants.

"Oh, this is Natasha. Natasha, this is Naina."

"Hi," she says, giving me a small wave. There's something sweet about her, and in another time or another headspace, I would be flirting with her, angling my body toward hers. But right now, she and David are standing too close for me to consider any kind of attraction, anything but apprehension.

"You both have 'N' names!" Christian says gleefully. It takes everything in me not to shoot him a death stare.

"I love your costume," I tell her. Perhaps dressing as a man-eating cheerleader would have been a better idea for tonight.

"Thanks," she says. "I love yours too."

"We were just talking about him the other day," David says to Natasha, who pushes a strand of hair from her face. "Bob Ross." He explains our conversation and how I joked about the costume. "Had no idea you'd actually do it, Naina!"

"Oh, I love that show," Natasha says, looking only at David. "The visuals are stellar."

My blood boils.

"Yeah, the *cinematography* is great," I say, interrupting their eye contact. David squints at me. I gulp my wine. "So, what do you do, Natasha?"

"I'm a creative director," she says, smiling and nodding.

"Wow," I say. "Seems like everyone is a creative director in this city!" The smoke is making me nauseous, yet I continue to inhale from the cigarette as if it's a prop.

Natasha doesn't break her smile. "What about you?" she asks. "What do you do?"

"I work in marketing." I take another gulp.

"Naina is a really amazing writer," David says. "She's been working on this fascinating essay—"

I shrug, cutting him off. "Eh. Who knows if that'll go anywhere."

Again, David squints at me. "She's been helping me write a short film, too."

"Oh yeah, you were saying you're really excited about it," Natasha says, touching his arm.

"I am. Hoping we can shoot it early next year."

Christian puts his hand on David's shoulder and shakes it encouragingly. I've stopped listening to the conversation.

"Need another drink," I say, interjecting and then

walking away, revolted by my own behavior toward Natasha.

I trudge back into the kitchen. I don't see any more wine bottles. Just beer and liquor. I pour myself a shot of tequila and throw it back.

On this alcohol-fueled tear, I see the truth: that I spent the past month telling myself a lie. My feelings for David *are* a big deal. Which is why I had such a petulant reaction to Natasha. I feel guilty for it, embarrassed. I hope no one noticed.

"One for me too, please."

Margot approaches me with a hopeful smile. I pour her a shot in a Solo cup, and she grimaces as she swallows.

"Horrible." She chokes.

"Can never get used to it," I reply.

"So, how's New York?" she asks me. "Since we first met, what? Last month? David's birthday?"

"Good," I say blandly, still stuck on what happened in the backyard. "Working. Making some new friends."

An awkward silence punctuates our conversation. I clear my throat.

"You and David have been hanging out a lot," she says.

At this point, I'm too drunk to obscure any of my feelings or refrain from sharing my thoughts. I look her in the eye. "We have been. I know he's your ex."

She smiles and nods, looking down at her shoes. "Yeah. Although it's not weird anymore."

"Do you guys ever talk?"

She laughs. "Sometimes. He's a good guy. He's a funny person. And generous."

"He is," I agree. "What was it like to date him?" I want to hear Margot's side of the story, but I quickly realize it sounds like I'm asking for a boyfriend Yelp review.

"Well," she says, pouring herself another shot and taking it, "he's kind of a slut."

I'm shocked by sweet Margot using the word *slut* to describe her ex-boyfriend. "What do you mean? Did he cheat on you or something?"

"Oh no, not that. Never. He's very loyal, *extremely*. I just couldn't get over the fact that any time we'd be at a party or at a show or whatever, there'd be at least two or three girls there that he'd fucked."

I nod, trying to understand why Margot feels comfortable enough to be so candid with me. She didn't have to answer my question. We barely know each other. Is she trying to warn me out of kindness? Or jealousy? Either way, she must think something is going on between David and me. And there *is* something going on, isn't there? Or maybe there isn't because he's outside in the backyard with Natasha.

"He did tell me that he's had, uh, sexual history with a lot of people in your circle," I say.

"Yeah. Like that girl he brought with him tonight, Natasha? They used to hook up, like, right after we broke up. He met her on a dating app, I think. She doesn't really fit into his life, though. She's humorless. I guess that's why she's a hookup."

I indulge in Margot's description of Natasha. But then guilt steadily tugs at me. Natasha is simply caught in the middle of my feelings toward a man. My annoyance with her suddenly feels like I am doing the worst possible job of cosplaying hetero.

But then I remember David's chest, and my nose pressed up against it, and the way he sleepily moans and sighs when he pulls my body closer to his, and annoyance transforms into rage. Like he brought Natasha just to hurt me, and I can't understand why. I feel like my only two choices are playing it cool or unleashing my anger, and both reactions seem disingenuous. I want to collapse, beat my fists on the ground, and beg David for an answer.

"We're not dating. Or hooking up. Just so you know," I tell Margot. I crack open a bottle of beer.

She nods. "I won't lie. I was curious. You seem cool and interesting, so. It wouldn't be a good look for him to come here with her if that were the case."

"So, what, he's got, like, a roster? Of women?" I ask.

"Basically. I'm not sure about now, but he did when I knew him. I mean, I was a little insecure when we dated, because it felt like before me, he'd sleep with *anyone*. We were already hooking up, and it felt like he was suddenly ready to have a girlfriend, and I was just *there*."

"That can't be true. He speaks really fondly of you."

Margot gives me a half-hearted smile. "Anyway, this is weird, right? Like why are we talking about David right now? I want to know more about you and your writing."

I remember Christian's comment about Margot being

a bad stand-up comic. In private defiance, I tell her, "I want to see you perform."

"Be careful what you wish for," she says, laughing.

David walks into the kitchen, searching for something. Or someone. He spots Margot and me. He approaches us, and my soul exits my body, I think, while they greet and hug each other. Guilty of talking about him, I'm now anticipating some sort of confrontation.

"I need to find Rana," she says. "She texted me a couple of minutes ago. Nice catching up with you, Naina." Margot leaves, and I take a swig of beer, foolishly hoping to both quell my nausea and give off an air of indifference.

"Heard you and Christian had a little dance break," David says.

"We did. It was fun. He's a fun dude."

"Need some water?" he asks me.

"I'm good," I lie. I am desperate for hydration. "Rana's here?"

"She's dressed as a fortune teller. She keeps going around telling people that someone in their life is betraying them. She's in a dark mood, I think."

"I should go find her. I'd love to hear what she has for me."

"Wait," David says, taking hold of my wrist. "I want to talk to you."

"Where's Natasha?" I ask.

"I don't know. Mingling?"

"Well, you should go find her," I say, attempting to leave.

"Whoa, Naina. What is this?" He holds my wrist tighter.

"What's what?" I ask.

"You seem like you're mad at me?"

"Why would I be mad?"

David runs his other hand through his hair. His watch beeps. It's midnight.

He strokes my hand with his thumb. "You were being weird outside . . ."

"I'm just drunk."

"Yeah, I can see that."

I avoid looking at him and drink my beer. I turn my gaze back to the fridge magnets.

He lets go of my wrist. "You *are* mad. Why?"

I sigh. "Okay, I'm annoyed. And I hate that you're pretending that you don't know why."

"Well, I want you to *tell* me. Is it Natasha?"

"Yes, that's why. *You* invited me to this party, and you show up here with, like, a model, and I'm confused because . . ." I'm not sure how to say what I want to say.

"Wait, what? We didn't come *together*. I ran into her here, and we were catching up. Except I was really hoping to be spending more time with you, but you ran off."

I am relieved, but I don't want to reveal it. I reacted impulsively, which was embarrassing. I wanted to be the only person David invited. I was terrified that he would go home with Natasha.

"Oh," I say.

"You're jealous," David says with a small, sympathetic

smile. As much as this enrages me, I'm charmed that he understands.

"Of course I'm jealous," I say. "We have . . . a thing."

"What, you and Natasha?" he jokes. I lightly punch his forearm, and he laughs before catching my hand and holding it. He reaches for the other one. We stand like that, him holding both of my hands, and I am ablaze.

David sighs. "Yeah. I know we do."

We continue to stand awkwardly, arms outstretched, hands linked. I avoid eye contact, biting the inside of my cheek, my gaze on the crease of his elbow. David refuses to look away, and when I finally give in and meet his eyes, he takes a step closer. "I like spending time with you," he says. "Writing together and holding each other accountable, talking, sleeping in the same bed. But I need you to *tell* me if you're into me."

My anger wilts. I can tell him how I really feel, and this can be solved.

But holding on to rage is too habitual for me to let it go this easily.

How obvious do I have to be? We text all the time, we share a bed, I told him about the nightmares I had about my mother. It feels like he's choosing to be oblivious.

"Naina, also," he continues, "I don't want to make you feel uncomfortable again or make assumptions—"

I cut him off. "You wouldn't be. You aren't."

He nods, reassured. "There's obviously . . . *tension* between us, but I also thought . . ."

"David, I do *like* you." The shock of admitting this, of opening something new between us, nearly sobers me up.

His face softens. I let myself look at him, at his eyes, his left and then his right. Something passes between us, intense and electric. I turn away.

"I mean, I wasn't sure if I liked you. I've never *liked* a *man*. But there's something between us. Isn't there? Am I crazy?"

David stares back at me, bewildered, his expression blank. "You're not crazy," he finally replies. But it's not enough.

"I feel like I'm having an identity crisis."

David's shoulders surrender into a slump. I feel an uneasy mix of relief and guilt, like I smashed a glass bottle to the floor. If I hadn't been so envious of Natasha, this conversation would not have happened. What will telling him this do to our friendship?

"I need a minute," I say, filling the silence between us. "The Natasha thing . . . I just need to go home." The emotional whiplash of being jealous, reevaluating my jealousy, and admitting to David how I really feel in quick succession—it is all too much. David starts to say something but reconsiders. He lets me go.

I abandon my drink, walk away, and find my coat on the couch, where Christian's sitting with his arm around a woman I've never seen before. "Whoa, Naina, you leaving?"

"Tired," I say. "Bye, Christian."

I call a car. When I arrive home, I throw up in my toilet.

VIII

I wake up terrifyingly hungover.

It's almost noon. Images from last night slowly reemerge in my pounding skull: the fury of seeing Natasha and David together, my strangely vulnerable conversation with Margot, and, *oh god, what I said to David.*

I groan and roll over to my side to check my phone. Only a missed call from my father. I swipe through social media. Christian posted a photo of him and David together. I try to find any indication of what David is thinking in his smile. He looks like he had a good time. Of course he did. Despite the crazy gay girl who confessed her feelings for him.

I discover and remember, both at once, that I posted a photo of myself in my costume. Sofia liked it and commented with a star-eyed emoji. I'm comforted by the familiarity of her presence, even in this innocuous way. I respond back with a painting emoji.

I work up the strength to drag myself to the kitchen. I swallow an insane amount of water. Jhanaki is in the living room crocheting and watching something.

"You're crocheting," I point out.

"I am," she responds, not looking away from the ball of yarn in her lap. "How was last night, Bob Ross?"

I shake my head. "Hungover."

"Sounds like it was a fun night."

"It was for a little bit. And then it wasn't. I wanted to be, like, Sean Paul drunk. But I got Tove Lo drunk."

"Uh-oh. David?"

I nod.

"What happened?"

I sink to the floor. Standing is beyond me right now. "It was complicated. He was hanging out with another woman at the party. And she was superhot. Like, she was *my type*. She wasn't his date, but I didn't know that so I confronted him. I don't know, it was very confusing."

"You should have stolen her away and made out with her in the bathroom. That would've been iconic."

"It would've been sloppy. Sloppier than it already was. I told him that I have feelings for him."

Jhanaki shoots up from her seat, crochet falling to the wayside, and clutches the back of the couch. "What did *he* say?"

"He said we have *tension*."

Jhanaki blows a raspberry. "No shit."

"Anyway, I'm going back to bed so I can sleep more and pretend last night didn't happen."

"Drink water!" she says, pointing at me.

"Don't worry, I am!" I reply, pointing back.

I grab a pack of saltines from the cupboard, ready to escape reality for deep sleep, when there's a knock.

I turn to Jhanaki, who shrugs. I open the door, and to my horror, it's David, looking worried and sweet, holding two cups of coffee.

I stand there, frozen and slack-jawed.

"Can I come in?"

I exchange a look with Jhanaki, who's staring at me with her eyes open wide, like she's watching a season finale.

"Sure," I say, opening the door wider.

"Hi, Jhanaki," he says at her back as she patters off into her room.

"Hi, David!" she replies while closing her door.

We sit at the kitchen counter.

"How're you feeling?" he asks me.

"Really hungover." I sip my cappuccino. "Thank you for this, the coffee."

He slips his bag off his shoulder and sets it on the ground. "Well, I want to talk about last night."

"Okay, yeah. We should probably do that."

He takes a deep breath. "I feel terrible. About how that went down. I . . . I'm sorry. Just so you know, I'm not sleeping with Natasha. We used to hook up, but we don't now."

I nod with relief, pleased that David felt the need to explain. Here was tacit acknowledgment that my interpretation of the situation was warranted, even if my reaction was not. I think back to what he told me about Margot and their incompatibility. I remember what Margot shared about running into David's exes and old hookups. I'm certain how I reacted was reminiscent of their dynamic. I'm discomfited by the thought of reminding him of Margot, yet I don't want to apologize.

David rubs his chest for a few moments, lost in thought, before speaking again. "But it made sense, the more I thought about it. How it must have looked. You and I have been spending all this time together and . . . cuddling? That's what we're doing, right? I like it a lot. If I'd known how you felt, really felt . . ."

I drink my cappuccino, still recovering from my embarrassment.

He pushes his coffee aside and rubs his thumbnail across his upper lip. "I said it last night at the party—I was looking to hang out with *you*. I feel a connection with you. I wasn't sure what to make of it. Especially because of the first time we met and how I put my foot in my mouth. I didn't want to say anything to you or talk about how I was feeling because I didn't want to look stupid in front of you. Again. That's fair, right? That's human, right?"

I sigh. We look at each other.

"It makes me sad that I hurt you last night, Naina. And I guess I'm also sad that you had feelings for me and didn't tell me."

"I didn't know what to say!" I say a little too loudly, feeling my headache intensify. "I didn't know *what* I was feeling. But I didn't think I needed to say anything. I thought it was obvious that getting close to you was a big deal for me. I even told you in Christian's car that I liked you."

The words tumble out before I can evaluate them. It's as if I'm peeling back layers I didn't know existed, revealing a tenderness I hadn't anticipated. Exposing myself like this—to both David and myself—is both liberating and unsettling.

David furrows his brows and fiddles with his fingers, his gaze fixed on his hands, an expression of combined shame and contemplation settling over his face.

I look at my own hands. "You can't blame me for not saying or clarifying anything when I haven't felt anything like this before, and I feel wrong about it and—"

"Why's it wrong?" he asks.

"It just feels wrong," I insist. "But that's not for you to deal with. That's for me to deal with."

"That's not true!" he says, thwacking the counter before composing himself. "I care about you and want to know what you're feeling and thinking. I want you to feel safe enough to tell me. I'm sorry if I didn't make you feel safe."

His apology hits me with unexpected force, this clear intention to make me feel protected. No one has ever expressed that kind of desire for me before.

We sit in silence, examining each other. I continue to sip my coffee, tasting nothing, resolute in hiding the whirlwind of emotions churning inside me. I've already shown too much.

"I feel the same way," he says, taking a deep breath.

"What do you mean?" I ask.

"I mean I really like you. *I like you.* I'm so attracted to you. I think you're wonderful, and beautiful, and so smart.

And ever since I met you, I've felt more excited than I have in a long time. I want to keep being around you and feeling that way."

I feel my face shifting, betraying me, unable to mask the feelings emerging beneath my anger.

He looks down, blushing but smirking. "I also, for the record, find you incredibly sexy, and sleeping in the same bed as you without doing anything has been the most insane and prolonged edging I've ever engaged in. I am desperate to be touching you at all times, if I'm being honest." He pauses. "But I think we can—we should—take things slow. You just got out of a relationship, and I know it's also weird—or maybe not weird but different?—because I'm a man. I guess my point is, I think we should just see how things go. Because I don't want to screw this up."

I close my eyes to make sense of what he's just said.

"First of all, it is very kind of you to say those things about me while I still have last night's wig glue stuck to my forehead. Second of all, if *I'm* being honest, I have been politely ignoring your morning wood, but I'm pleased to know I should take it personally."

He laughs and shakes his head. "All right, that's enough."

I keep going. "I want to keep being around you, too. And I also want to do this right. And that takes time," I tell him.

David gives my hand a gentle squeeze. "Of course, you want to do everything *right*. We can try. Be intentional."

I squeeze his hand back. He kisses my knuckles, and I hold in a gasp. The feeling of his lips on my skin sends a flood of warmth through my body. I am engulfed in astonishment.

He clears his throat. "I have to go to the gym now, and you should probably go back to bed. I'm going to text you later. To make plans. To be around each other." He smiles, his eyebrows scrunched. I stand up to walk him out.

"Thank you for the coffee," I say, stalling. "And for coming by to talk."

"Thanks for letting me." He lingers by the door, leaning against the frame, his mouth growing into a grin.

What I know how to do with David is stretch our evenings out, prolonging the inevitable: him in my bed, the comforting safety of his embrace, his chest pressed into mine. The intimacy of our sleepy murmurs, his fingers gently stroking my hair. Once, I woke up with my mouth pushed against the soft inner curve of his bicep, and the impulse to kiss him was almost overwhelming. Now, with everything said between us, I wonder how we proceed.

David scans my face, no longer smiling but inching closer until his mouth is on mine in a sudden, urgent kiss. Heat unfurls through me, the softness and fullness of his lips turning into something real, into something I could never forget. He cradles my chin, I reach for the back of his neck, and I dread the moment it will end. As his tongue gently explores my mouth, the abrupt beep of his watch cuts through the moment. It's noon.

"Okay, I should go," he says, his voice barely above a whisper. "Slow." He nods as if reminding himself.

I'm shy, still reeling from the kiss. "Have a nice day. Tell Christian I said hi."

"I will."

In the aftermath, we've both lost the ability to say anything real. A surge of emotion nearly compels me to pull him back in, but I keep my arms glued to my sides, aware that the moment is fragile.

He leaves. I close the door.

"Shit," I mutter to myself as Jhanaki comes out of her bedroom.

"I wasn't trying to eavesdrop, but it got really quiet there at the end," she says, her voice low.

I look at her, my fingers on my lips.

"Oh *shit*," she says.

IX

It's been three days since we kissed, and naturally I can't stop thinking about David. We've texted, but we haven't seen each other. I'm exhausting my sounding boards: Jhanaki and I processed my last conversation with David from all possible angles. I took Chloe out for happy hour drinks, where I ordered a Diet Coke, my stomach still turning at the thought of alcohol.

"What is the definition of 'taking it slow'? I wonder if he knows what he wants," Chloe questioned. "Or is he stalling?" I bit my straw instead of telling Chloe what I was thinking: that, truthfully, I don't know exactly what I want and am grateful I have some latitude to figure it out with him.

On my way back to Brooklyn after a brutal day at work, I shoot Jordan a text—*FaceTime tonight?* When I get home, I delay our conversation by taking a long shower. I know he's going to chide me for keeping him in the dark and that I deserve it. I scrub my scalp twice, working the pads of my fingers through my hair and allowing the steam to make me woozy. Letting hot water pour over my body has always been my pregame ritual before any nerve-wracking event.

I throw the duvet over me and sink into the pillows as I wait for Jordan to pick up. When he does, we greet each other with goofy faces, then burst into laughter. It's been weeks since we last spoke. It's mostly my fault.

"You've been busy." He tries to sound light, but I can tell he's veiling hurt at not having heard from me in so long.

"Yeah, it's true. I miss you." I want to be casual, but I feel the story bursting at the seams. I'm equally eager to confess what I haven't told him and nervous about what it might mean to bring my relationship with David to light within the context of my old life, my Chicago life.

"Well, what's up?"

"It's about David," I say, biting my lip, preventing myself from smiling.

"What's that cheeky smile?" Jordan asks. "What did you do?"

I divulge the details of the past few weeks—the cuddling, Halloween night, the showing up at my door with coffee. I get through everything without questions—just Jordan's empathetic gasps and exclamations of disbelief. When I reach the part about the kiss, he yelps and shakes his phone.

"I knew it!" he howls. "I *called* it!"

We laugh and swoon together.

"So what, are you gonna be like—'actually, let's just date'? Or are you going to go with the flow? *His* flow?"

"I don't know," I confess. "There's a part of me that feels almost . . . shy? About asking what he means by 'take it slow.' As if I'm just supposed to know what that means. And if I admit that I don't, it could ruin it."

Jordan clicks his tongue. "Asking for clarity won't ruin anything. And if it does, then he's not the one."

"Maybe I'm accepting the ambiguity, as much as it scares me, because *I* don't know what I want," I admit.

Jordan considers this hypothesis. "That would make sense. You did just get out of a relationship. But eventually you guys have to figure out what you are to each other. What is the point of all of this talking if not?"

I groan. I know Jordan is right. And as much as I want to process this with David—to talk it out like my essay or his film—I feel nervous at the thought of dissecting something so real, so personal.

"So, when're you seeing him again?" Jordan asks, setting his phone down to brush his teeth.

"Tomorrow."

"Let me know how it goes. And follow your heart," he croaks, toothpaste foaming in his mouth.

"Terrible advice. That's never worked for anyone."

David opens his front door.

For the past week, I've found myself thinking about him constantly—wondering what he'd say about my cooking, whether he'd approve of my choice of shallots over white onions. When I decided to bike home instead of taking the train, I imagined us cycling together to the farmer's market. While cringing at a street performer, I thought about his likely reaction—his belief that true artistry means putting yourself out there.

These little fantasies started to scare me over the past few days. When did I let myself go all-in on this, and am I losing my sense of self to my feelings for him? Without even fully processing what it means that, all of a sudden, I'm attracted to a *man*? When I'd finally gotten to a place where I no longer felt like I wasn't "queer enough"? Am I absorbing his lens and applying it to my life, erasing my own perspective?

I am timid standing in front of him, unsure of what to do with my body.

"Sorry, one minute." He waves both hands at me in yellow dish gloves as he approaches and leans down to peck my cheek.

Breathless, I walk past him into the living room and sit on his couch. He's cleaning the kitchen and talking to me about his week—a meeting with a clueless client whose demands made no technical sense, an argument with Rana about the dishes in the sink that he's doing now, a sleepless night helping a friend shoot a short. He seems normal. How can he be so normal after what happened this weekend?

I notice he cut his hair. I'd made a comment, the day

before the Halloween party, about how long it had gotten. Now, his dark curls sit neatly on top of his head, cropped short, tapering down at the sides.

"What about you?" he asks. "How's your week been?"

"Fine," I say, my eyes on the little table where we had our first dinner. "I sent those pitches out finally."

"What!" he says, dropping a pan in the sink. "Naina, that's huge! I'm so proud of you!"

I feel stupidly giddy. I'd been motivated to pitch my essay because David had been so encouraging. But he already approved of me—me sending a few emails doesn't change anything. What else did I possibly have to prove?

"Thanks," I say. "But I guess that means I technically have nothing to work on tonight. I can read your latest draft if you want."

"We should celebrate," he says, slipping the gloves off and opening the fridge with gusto. "Okay, so there's no champagne, but we *do* have the champagne of beers. Want one?"

He hands me a cold Miller High Life. "I'm not drinking this week." I pass it back to him. "I'm still, uh . . . *recovering.*"

He chuckles and sits on the couch beside me, wiping his palms down the front of his pants, then reaching up to cup my chin. "I've never seen you that drunk before. It was bad, huh?"

I laugh at myself, covering my eyes with my hands.

"What got into you? Why'd you drink so much?"

"I guess I was nervous. I mean, I usually am before parties, but . . . I guess I was nervous to see you."

He smirks. "Me? For what? We see each other all the time and you're never nervous."

I chew on my lip.

He raises his eyebrows. "Wait, do I make you nervous?"

"Maybe," I tease.

"Sometimes you make me nervous," he says, taking my bid and leaning his forehead toward mine. "When you give me those eyes."

"What eyes?"

"You know," he replies, making puppy dog eyes at me. "*Those* eyes."

I reach out, my fingertips finding their way to the side of his face, and he leans his cheek into my hand. Blood rushes to my head. I am nervous, yes, but despite it, I shift my knees and lean in to kiss him.

I am hungry to return to the exact moment of our first kiss, but as soon as our tongues brush against each other, I know this is different, needier, less constrained. He slowly pushes me down on the couch, cradling my head, until we're both lying down and he is beside me. I feel his ring pressed up against my face, cold and metallic, and I follow the urge to put his fingers in my mouth. He's surprised when I do, which only encourages me more. I glide my tongue between his fingers.

A door upstairs opens, then shuts. We freeze.

"Should we go to my room?" he whispers to me. I smile and nod. He plants a soft kiss on my mouth.

He holds my hand and leads me up the stairs. I've been in his room multiple times, but never like this—never *for* this.

I stand with my back pressed against the wall while he shuts the door, presenting myself as ready for whatever will happen next. In two swift strides, he's in front of me, an arm wrapping around my waist. "Come here," he grumbles, pulling me onto the bed with more force than I expect but not more than I need. I am greedy for his attention and satisfied that I'm getting what I want. I lie on top of him, my hair framing his face and my legs straddling his right thigh. He holds my hips with both hands and gently rocks me back and forth, the ridge in my jeans announcing itself loudly. "How's that feel?" he whispers in my ear, and the sensation of his breath is almost enough to make me crest. I'm straining to focus, to make it last, and all I can utter in response is "It feels so good." I am in disbelief at being with David in this way, at how my body feels on top of his. I moan into his mouth without worrying about who might hear.

I stop kissing him to smell his neck—unabashedly, indulgently. I tug the skin on his throat with my teeth. I'd questioned if I'd know what to do when it came to this, but now that we're here, it feels obvious. Humans are humans. Touch is touch. I know how to kiss. I know how to touch.

"You smell incredible," I say, the skin of his neck still between my lips.

"You do too," he whispers back. "You always do." He turns to kiss my jaw. "I am so turned on by the way you smell. I want every part of you in my mouth."

I gasp, kissing him back. He flips me over onto my back and holds himself over me.

He runs his fingers down my sternum. I take his hand and urge him to touch my chest, *more*, *harder*, and he spreads his palm around my breast, gently squeezing and brushing his thumb over the fabric covering my nipple, calling attention to the throbbing in between my thighs. He pulls my top off over my head, and I tug at his T-shirt, slipping it off to reveal his bare chest, covered in dark hair. We take each other in, hands all over each other's bodies, entirely consumed by the moment. I undo his fly, releasing the strain of his erection, but before I can go further, he's growling, tonguing my breast through the cotton of my bra and then skillfully unhooking it. A nervousness creeps into my body—less apprehension, more uncertainty—and he licks my neck. None of this is new to me, but it's new with David, new with him. He stops for a moment to gaze at me, and I witness an expression I've never seen from him before. *Hunger.*

I love seeing him like this. I watch him watch me while I unbutton my jeans and wriggle my way out of them, kicking them off the bed.

Immediately, his hand is in between my thighs, and we sigh in unison, both delighted by how wet I am. He pushes my underwear to the side, inspecting. I writhe against his fingers, desperate.

He moves his head down my torso, pushing my legs apart, tickling my skin with his hair. I'm aching to have his mouth on me, feeling like we could never be close enough. He kisses the inner part of my thighs, savoring every part of me.

I lift myself up onto my elbows, looking down at him. "Touch me," I beg. "Please."

Not breaking eye contact, he gently strokes my clit with his index finger, causing me to buck my hips. I want more. He kisses my entrance lightly, tormenting me, watching me squirm against him, until finally, he licks.

"I've wanted to taste you since I walked in here and found you on my bed. The first time we met."

My mind scans back through the times I've been in this room, but I can't latch on to thoughts, just the sensation of his tongue, dragging, probing, seeking.

"My very belated birthday present," he says as if addressing my whole being, answering all of my questions, through this conversation between my legs.

I melt into the softness of his mouth on me. He slides a finger inside of me, then two.

I grip his head in between my thighs. "Sorry," I gasp, and he comes back up to kiss me, his mouth glistening and swollen. "What're you sorry for?" He smiles, pleased with himself. He brushes his fingers against my lips, enraptured.

"I'm going to take forever to come," I admit, pressing my palms against my eyes. He gently pulls my hands off my face.

"Is that a challenge?" he asks.

We are lying on our sides now, facing each other. He takes his pants off, then his briefs, keeping his eyes on me. I am locked in, hoping my gaze will communicate what I want it to: *Yes, yes. More, more.*

He strokes himself with his right hand, and I'm watching him, rapt. I've never been this close to a dick before. I like how his looks. He returns my gaze, steady and intent. "Tell me what you want, Naina."

"I want you. I just don't know how I want you," I answer. I kiss him, more sloppily than before, spit reaching my chin. He whispers into my ear, "You can have me however you want."

I reach for his dick, surprised by the weight of it in my palm. How velvety he feels. His head rolls back as I run my thumb along the vein. He groans, then puts his hand on top of mine. "Like this." He shows me.

"Will you fuck me?" I ask, fighting off my nerves and forcing myself to stay out of my head.

He traces a finger down my side, the most delicate gesture since we stepped into his room. "We can try, and I'll stop if you don't like it. How does that sound?"

I'm touched and relieved and turned on all at once, a decidedly new combination of feelings for me. I kiss him. He opens his nightstand drawer and pulls a condom out, tearing it open and rolling it on. I watch him, nearly clinical in my observation.

I lie back, and he braces himself over me. "You're in charge, okay?" he says, cupping my jaw and making direct eye contact. "Okay," I whisper in response as I guide his dick to my entrance. He pushes himself inside of me, slowly, watching my face for a reaction. I nod for him to keep going. He does, hesitantly, and his breathing goes shallow. He's trying not to lose himself. I feel full in the most pleasurable way, but as he begins to thrust harder, I wince.

"Can you stop?" I whimper. He does, pulling himself out abruptly.

"I'm . . . sorry," I say. "This is just very intense." It is an emotional whirlwind, to have him inside of me. I don't want to think about what it means for *me* to be having sex with a man. I want to lose myself to the genuine pleasure of the experience, not to unnecessary mental gymnastics.

"Don't apologize," he says, squeezing my hand. "It is for me too. Why don't I hold you for a bit?" he asks.

"Please," I whisper.

He spoons me—something we've done before, but never like this—and he sighs into my neck. I kiss the inner part of his arm as many times as I possibly can.

We breathe together for a handful of minutes. I'm having a private moment of disbelief lying next to him: pleased with myself, surprised, and shocked all at once. I replay the events so they feel real, reminding myself *that actually just happened.*

I take his hand and place it between my thighs. He starts to move his fingers in a gentle circle. I reach back to hold his face into my neck, unable to be completely satisfied, feeling like we can never be close enough.

"I want to try again," I say.

"Get another condom," he tells me.

I hand it to him, but he passes it back to me.

"You do it. You show me how you want it."

I rip the foil packet, heady with a sense of control, and slide it over him.

This time he slides himself inside of me while I straddle him. It's easier to relax now. I breathe deeply, feeling a surge of pleasure with each exhale. My shoulders fall to his chest while he lifts my hips up and down. He groans my name into my neck over and over again, still circling his fingers on my clit, asking me if it feels good, if I'm getting what I want.

"I *need* this," I say, close to a sob, desire radiating through me as he thrusts fervently. He greedily squeezes my hips and growls. My body trembles, desperate to reach orgasm. As I come, I dissolve into the rush, and everything disappears. David follows, his moans climbing into an entranced rhythm.

When we are finished, he maneuvers his body so it's enclosed around mine, his dick still inside of me.

"Did you like it?" he asks through heavy breaths.

"Could you not tell?" I whisper back, my mind fully turned to mush.

He squeezes me against him. "I want you to tell me."

"I liked fucking you so much," I say, resting my head in the crook of his neck, feeling him smile in response.

"Your face fits perfectly in there," he says, pressing his cheek against my head.

"I'll just live here now," I say. "In the crook."

He laughs. "Whenever I need you close, I'll just tell you to come home."

I wake up before David, shocked into consciousness by the bliss of having his naked body enveloping mine.

He is not a discreet sleeper. He snores. His breathing is more like a soft whistling. The air from his nose tickles the skin behind my ear. Having his limbs wrapped around mine causes me to indulge in flashbacks of the sex we had. All the different kinds—moving from exploratory to depraved, gentle to impassioned, relaxed to borderline athletic. He picked me up, he caressed me, he told me how beautiful my body is and the mess he wanted to make of it.

He is no longer just my friend.

His pattern of breathing changes. He stirs, moving his face in my hair. My butt is pressed up against him. We're all soft and sticky. I loosen myself from his grip and turn into him, tucking my leg between his thighs.

"David," I say, holding his face, tracing his lips with my thumb, "are you awake?"

He grumbles. "No."

"I have to go to work."

"What time is it?"

"I think seven. Your watch beeped."

"My alarm goes off at seven thirty. Don't go yet." He squeezes me against him, cupping my butt in his hand.

"I need to shower. And eat."

"Shower with me. We'll get breakfast."

"My laptop is at home," I groan.

David finally opens his eyes, planting a kiss on my nose. "What if you called in sick?"

"Call in sick just so we can sleep in?"

"Call in sick so we can sleep in, get breakfast, go for a walk. Then have sex again. So much of it. If you want," he says. The fluttering in my stomach shifts to the space in between my legs, now sore but still insatiable.

The thought of having David all to myself for an entire day feels like something out of a dream. Here is a person who I want like this, who wants me back like this.

"Look." He traces the line of my jaw. "If this sways your decision: I'm going out of town in a couple of days, for that backpacking trip in Utah. Two weeks without seeing each other and little to no cell service. Maybe we deserve some extra time together."

I wince inwardly. I vaguely recall him mentioning these plans during one of our late-night writing sessions, a reunion of sorts with one of his high school buddies. But being reminded of them now, they seem somehow unfair. How can David be gone so soon after this drastic shift in our relationship? I will miss him. I will want him to come back so we can pick up where we leave off.

"Where's my phone?" I say, pulling his arm off me. "I'll email Alice."

X

David leaves for his trip. He sends a selfie from his early morning flight, instructing me not to miss him too much. After a week of his absence, I'm still waiting to hear from him again. He warned me communication would be spotty, but I'm both surprised and irritated by the silence. I'd be happy to receive anything: one cliché nature photo, a "thinking of you" message. Proof that what happened between us is leading us somewhere. Yet I refuse to text him. He was inside of *me*, after all. I shouldn't have to be the one to reach out, to profess my longing.

That's not very bell hooks of you, Jordan texts me. I ignore it. Instead, I spiral and regress. I fall out of my writing habit. I have two too many glasses of wine with Chloe and end up with a Wednesday hangover. I snap at Jhanaki about the teens doing drugs and having sex on the TV too loudly.

To go from feeling so connected to David to feeling untethered destabilizes me. *Why didn't I ask him what we are to each other before he left?* Being in my bed alone is torture.

I'm seriously considering that he was a figment of my imagination, I text Jordan.

See, this is why I need to meet him. Verify he's made of flesh and bones, he responds.

I don't want to think of myself differently simply for liking David, but I do, even if no one else does. And when he's not here, real, I start to hate myself for it. Right or wrong, I take his silence as evidence that my feelings are in vain, a form of self-betrayal.

I wake up to a knock at my front door. My cortisol spikes, driving a nervous thump in my chest.

It's nine in the evening, and I'm home alone. Feeling sorry for myself, I had put myself to bed without dinner and only scrolling for sustenance.

I pull on pajama pants, look through the peephole, and, like some kind of apparition, see Sofia staring down at her shoes, her bag slung over her shoulder.

I fling the door open, wondering if my eyes are working correctly. They are.

"Sofia," I say. "What're you doing here?" I take a step back, then forward again.

"Your address," she says, right hand scratching the back of her neck, her nervous tic. "It was on the package you sent me. My sweatshirt."

This doesn't answer my question. Why did—how

could—Sofia turn up unannounced to New York? To *my apartment*?

I say this out loud, attempting to disguise how I feel: "I didn't think you would . . . surprise me like this."

"I'm here for a conference." She throws up her hands, eager to clarify she didn't get on a flight to see me. "I landed a few hours ago, dropped off my things at my hotel, and then just . . . I should have texted. Or called."

Sofia fills my silence with more explanation, clearly hoping to ease my shock. "I just thought, since we were in contact . . . Naina, I miss you." She looks down, smiling to herself shyly, and it's so obvious that showing up to my apartment is not about accosting me—it's an act of love. In my tender state, this feels welcome.

"Sit," I tell her, waving her in and motioning to the barstool. I give her a glass of water.

Sofia and I look at each other in silence for a few moments, her fidgeting with her moldavite bracelet, me standing with my arms crossed, leaning against the kitchen counter.

"I need to tell you something." It's not ripping off the Band-Aid as much as it is suddenly exposing a wound to open air. I speak cautiously, enunciating every word in case I need to catch myself. "I'm kind of seeing someone."

Sofia's face falls. She is a confident, outspoken, strong person. But she has never been too good for a poker face. I know what I am about to tell her will upset her, and I will have to brave the conversation.

"It's sort of new," I continue, looking away. "And I'm

sorry if . . . I guess I don't know why you're here or if it's because you want . . . but I do have feelings for someone else, Sofia."

She nods, gritting her teeth, fingering her bracelet. She eventually throws her hands up.

"I'm an idiot," she says through a painful laugh.

"You're not."

"We left in such a bad place, and then it started feeling so much less bad. And I told myself that if I was going to be here, in New York, I should at least try. To see you." Her shoulders drop. "So, who is she?"

I brace myself against the pronouns. "His name is David."

Confusion, then disbelief, then something I've never seen before sweep across Sofia's face. Her spine straightens again.

"Wow," she says, her tone notably sour. "We've been broken up for three months, and now you're fucking men."

Men, she says, as if I've committed an act of barbarism.

"He's a friend," I respond, which is true—or was true—but still evasive. I want to ease into honesty. She is minutes away from knowing everything, and her obliviousness is still precious to me.

She takes a breath, coming down from her outburst. Her tone is gentler now. "You can date whoever you want. Obviously." A deep sigh. "Just . . . why didn't you tell me you were seeing other people?"

I suddenly feel bad for pestering Jordan to make sure knowledge of David didn't get back to her. I was so paranoid about how she'd respond that it led us to this moment.

Her right knee bounces up and down. "I feel like such a fucking idiot showing up here—"

"Sofia, I didn't tell you because it didn't seem necessary. Why do you still feel like you have some kind of *ownership* of me? I'm a human being—"

"I love you, Naina," she snaps.

"You're supposed to *ask* before you show up like this," I insist, shaking my hands at her, gritting my teeth.

"It was a grand gesture," she mumbles. She holds her head in her palms. "And I already had a plane ticket."

I sigh, attempting to ease my anxiety. "I get it," I reply. "I get why you did it."

"But you wish I didn't."

"That's a simple and unfair way of putting it," I say, scrunching up my face defensively.

"How'd you meet him?"

"Through Jordan. They have mutual friends. Then we became friends."

"You have straight friends now?"

"Sofia."

"So you've fucked him."

I accept there's no way of avoiding this.

"We've had sex, yes," I say, attempting to veil my guilt. I know I don't owe her this, but for some reason, I want to witness her hearing me say the words. If I can tell Sofia about David, then maybe both things can be true: that I was in love with a woman—this woman—and that I am also falling for a man. "We were friends, but then it felt like there was something more between us. And we had sex." There it is: the truth, or at least the beginning of it.

She nods.

"If I'm being honest," I say. "There have been so many moments where I missed you and our life in Chicago. When I met him—David—it finally felt like I was moving on. But he's been away, traveling, and I am all in my head about it. About what it is I'm doing with him and what it says about me."

Sofia shakes her head.

It's a relief to bare the truth to the person who has helped me work through so many of my identity crises. But she's staring at something in front of her, avoiding eye contact with me, making that pinched expression of hers to prevent herself from crying.

"How long are you here for?" I ask her, feeling pained.

"Three days."

We fall silent. The radiator switches on, filling the room with its humming.

"Maybe we should sort this out," I say, an attempt to take the lead between us for once.

"Sort what out?"

"This, us," I say. "So maybe we can have some closure."

"Naina," Sofia pleads, "are we actually going to sort this out? Or are you just going to do what you always do? You act like you're the victim of this relationship, but you're not. And I'm not saying I am, either. But you act like I have some kind of hold over you when in fact you just . . . you refuse to ask for what you want. And somehow that's *my fault*."

"I've been following your lead all these years," I retort. "I've *never* been able to—"

"Come on," Sofia says, holding her hand up. "*Follow- ing my lead?* Naina, I'm just as clueless as you are. I'm figuring my life out, too. But this is who I am—I make decisions and go for it. I thought you loved me for that, for me. And then suddenly *you* made this *one huge* decision to leave Chicago and come here, and it's like you've cut me out. All these years I've tried to be there for you, push you to *choose something* for yourself, and you turn around and slap me in the fucking face and disappear."

A threatening pressure forms behind my eyes. I look away from Sofia.

"See?" she says. "This is what I mean. You can't even look at me."

"You don't understand," I snap.

"What don't I understand?"

"I've always been that way, yes. I'm trying not to be anymore. I hate how nothing's in my control. I think when my mom died, I decided that if dying is inevitable and I can't dictate the terms of my life or how anything pans out, it's better to let other people decide for me."

Sofia curls her lip and turns her hand into a fist, press- ing her knuckles against the counter.

I'm holding back tears now, choking on my words. "I know I hurt you. I'm not trying to make this about me. I'm just explaining what I learned about myself from being with you, and it's one of the biggest reasons I left Chicago. I'm stuck in some fucking pattern, Sofia. I'm good at avoiding emotional accountability. But I don't want to be like this anymore." I think of David, of telling him the truth the morning after the Halloween party. "I am trying. I am."

Sofia puts her hand to her forehead and lets out a sharp laugh. "I can't believe it. That's all I wanted from you this entire time. And now I have it, but not you."

"Because it's over," I say.

"I know," she says.

She bounces her knee, shaking her head, refusing to look at me. "I'm honestly impressed you're fucking a guy," she spits. "I don't get it, but at least you chose something for yourself instead of being a sheep and then blaming someone else for your indecision."

"You hate men. You're not impressed; you're disgusted—"

"Oh please, I don't *hate* men. *You* hate men."

"I clearly don't," I respond.

"Well. He must be good," Sofia says, laughing caustically.

"He's a good person," I say, taking a deep breath. "And we have good chemistry. I care about him."

Sofia raises her eyebrows and draws closer to me, her voice laced with curiosity. "Really? You have good chemistry?"

I stare at her face, those sharp, demanding blue eyes. Her question is obviously rhetorical but also a challenge. Sofia and I had excellent chemistry too, once.

The space between us shrinks as she stands up from the barstool. Her throat is at eye level with me. She tilts her chin down, her lower lip unfolding slightly, revealing her bottom teeth. "How good?" she whispers, her breath hot against my ear. I am resistant to the moment but wickedly tempted, realizing our anger is morphing into something else, something I recognize. Historically, we fight and then fuck, our vulnerability leaving us both aching for connection.

"I'm here now," she whispers. "If you want me to leave, I'll leave."

"You don't need to leave," I reply.

"Right," she says, bringing her palm to my cheek. Like muscle memory, I place my hands on her waist, and we kiss.

Her tongue brushes against my lips urgently, and I raise my hips to sit on the kitchen counter. She kisses my chest and slips my T-shirt over my head. I wrap my legs around hers, a swell of excitement washing over me as her fingers gently but adamantly move between my thighs, her face pressed against my breasts.

"Is this what you want?" she asks, her hot breath warming my bare nipple, her cheek sticky against my skin.

"Don't ask me that," I whimper.

"Tell me," she demands, moving her hand to my neck, cupping my throat.

"Yes," I say, refusing to interrogate why.

She trails her tongue up my neck and kisses me again, fervently, her mouth all over my mouth, saliva finding its way to the tip of my nose. Her fingers are now closer to where my body begs for release.

I wrap my legs around her right thigh, squeezing, pressing myself against her palm. "Not yet," she whispers in my ear. I slide off the counter and lead her to the couch.

Sofia pulls her sweater off in one swift motion, then the T-shirt underneath, and I tug her body onto mine. We sloppily press our mouths together. I ask her to touch me, speaking into her lips, and she ignores me. I repeat myself, begging, and she pinches my left nipple. I moan.

In a flurry of emotion, I hold her head in my hands and direct it where I want her. She looks up at me and scoffs. "Please," I whisper. She smirks and finally concedes.

Her mouth latches on, and I lose it. My body surrenders itself to pleasure, like a last meal before death.

I'm splayed on top of Sofia. "I can't believe we did that," I say.

"It's only me." She tugs my earlobe affectionately.

"I know."

Our breathing is synchronized, our skin sticky and sour. I feel like I did something wrong, but I don't know if I did. I thought I might distract myself from my obsessive looping about David—remind myself that I exist outside the context of him—but I don't know if I did.

"It's fucked up," Sofia says. "All of this."

"I'm sorry," I say. "It was cold, the way I ended things with you. I just leaned on you, then resented you for it. It's unfair. I was being unfair."

Sofia sighs and rubs her face.

"I didn't know you were attracted to men," she mutters.

"Me neither. But does it matter?"

"Yes. Because the only thing I ever really wanted was to know you."

"You don't feel like you know me?"

"Only sometimes." She sighs.

I only sometimes know myself.

"What about me?" Sofia asks. "Do you feel like you know me?"

"I do. But sometimes I couldn't see you clearly because I was caught up in my own bullshit."

I move my fingers through her hair, and she exhales.

"I shouldn't have turned up here. I thought it would be romantic."

"It kind of was." I poke her cheek, and she laughs.

"Do you have feelings-feelings for him?" she asks hesitantly. "David?" My heartbeat soars, tapping against the underside of my chest.

"Do you really want me to answer that?"

"I want to know. Even if it's difficult. Even if it's fucked up."

"Yes," I whisper.

"Do you want to be with him?"

"I think so. I do."

"So you're a human being with feelings," Sofia says.

"It's nice to see, even if they're not for me. I feel like you used to be so much more guarded."

I play with a strand of her hair, twisting it around my finger. "I had feelings for you. I didn't know what to do with them. I'm sorry I hurt you."

Her chest expands, and she releases the air with a deep moan. "I'm sorry, too," she says.

I shift my body. "We probably shouldn't have sex again."

"Definitely not."

She pats my shoulder, motioning for me to sit up. I take my weight off her, and we slouch together on the couch, naked, legs outstretched.

"I go in between hating you and missing you. All. The. Time," she says.

I bury my head in a cushion and stay like that for a few moments, my nose bent upward, my breath moving like waves. I think about David. How much I miss him, how badly I want to hear from him, and, most worryingly, how things could be different with him than they were with Sofia. If I let them be. But without him standing in front of me, it is difficult to envision.

I turn and press my face into Sofia's bony shoulder, determined to say goodbye but not to shed a tear.

She holds my head to her, and I feel her body shake gently with her tears. "Fine," she whispers. "I'll cry for the both of us."

XI

When Sofia leaves, David's absence fills my apartment. I feel like a teenager, at the mercy of my feelings, somehow only able to access anger or devastation.

His name is like a mantra trapped in my head. I am nearly sick with emotion. Seeing Sofia only solidified how much I want him, in a full, complete way. Seeing Sofia, I was forced to be brave and admit I have feelings for *him*. I could reveal that I want more.

I give myself permission to continue being courageous. I start typing David a text message: *How are you? When you're back from your trip, I would love to see you and discuss more about us.*

I wince at the words *love* and *discuss*—what a strange tone of formality—and try again: *Hi. How are you? When you're back from your trip, let me know if you want to hang out and talk.*

I hit send, realizing after I do that my message sounds ominous. My chest tightens, and I take a deep inhale, the breath reaching down to my pelvic floor. I exhale like I'm letting air out of a balloon, slowly as not to startle.

An image appears: David lying next to me, his body curling around mine, his thumb stroking my hip bone. I shake my head, as if to make the memory disappear, at least until I know what happens next.

I distract myself with things that are good for me: working on another essay, watching television so I can discuss something with Jhanaki later, making an unnecessarily elaborate dinner—but even chopping herbs for the salad dressing brings me back to David. I clean the entire apartment, scrubbing away at the kitchen backsplash to EDM, hoping the computer-generated nonsense will dampen my tendency to spiral.

I could be thinking about other things right now, more important things, like my future or social injustices or global crises. But to resist the tug toward David—the way I feel when I'm with him, the thoughts I have of him, the desire I feel for him—only pulls me in deeper.

He texts me back as I'm lighting a candle, settling into the relief of a disinfected apartment. When I see his name on my phone, I almost try to fool myself out of a genuine reaction. As if I hadn't been checking it every twenty minutes, I place the screen face down. I stare at the flame, watching it dance, trying to prove detachment to myself. I catch a whiff of sandalwood. Of course it smells like David.

I wait two minutes before I read his message.

David: Hey! I just got back. Are you around tonight?

I type out a *yes* and hit send.

I wait for David at a bar near my apartment. He's fifteen minutes late. While I stew in my impatience, I ask the bartender for a shot, and she clears the glass before David arrives.

Calling him and asking where he is seems desperate, but I do it anyway.

He answers the phone quickly, shouting, "Hello? Sorry, I'm running late. I'm biking right now. It's very windy and cold, and it started raining. I'll be there soon." The wind whooshes through his words, breaking his speech.

He bursts into the bar, searching for me. I wave at him. His hair is sopping and shiny. He unzips his jacket, sprinkling droplets of water on the floor and into my lap.

"Hi." He sighs, pulling me into a wet hug. He kisses me on the mouth, and I am so close to forgetting my intentions to have a talk. "Sorry about that."

"Oh, it's all good," I respond, clearing my throat.

"I wish I had a towel or something," he says, running his fingers through his hair. He pulls the barstool closer to his body, and it screeches across the floor.

"We can ask the bartender."

He waves his hand, *it's fine*. We get two beers.

"How was your trip?" I ask.

"It was . . . very needed," he says with a sigh. I can see it on him, that inexplicable change that happens to a person after genuinely restorative time away. His skin is lush, his eyes bright, his attention immovable.

"I'm sorry I didn't reach out," he adds, hesitant. "I wasn't in the space to text a lot. And any time I had a moment to talk on the phone, there was no service. But I'm happy to be back, and to see you," he says, squeezing my thigh.

Intellectually, I understand why I didn't hear from David. I just hadn't expected to feel so strongly for him in his absence, so in my head about our relationship, so *overcome*.

And amidst all these intense emotions, I'd slept with my ex. I had been unfairly resentful toward David to cope with the ferocity of my own feelings, confused and frustrated with not knowing what was next for us. But the reality was I had done something questionable.

"That's okay." I smile. "I understand. But I did miss you, and . . . I don't know, not hearing from you—truthfully, it didn't make me feel good."

David reaches for my hand. "I thought about you a lot," he whispers, his features soft. "And I was excited to see you again."

My heart sinks, and I shift in my seat, unable to look him in the eye. There is no good time to tell him this. I pull my hand away. "All the missing you and not hearing from you, it fucked with my head, I think. And there's something I have to tell you."

I notice a flash of concern on his face before he nods for me to go on.

"I saw my ex. Sofia."

David doesn't seem too disturbed by this information, which is both endearing and unnerving. I brace myself before telling him more.

"She was in town and showed up unannounced. And . . . we had sex. It was *breakup sex*. We ended things, once and for all. Like we talked everything through and got closure. It's over. I wanted to tell you all this because I owe it to you after everything."

"You don't owe me anything," David says, and I feel a little piece of my soul break. He asks the bartender for a glass of water.

I touch his arm. "No, but . . . I do. I owe you respect and honesty. I mean, we were *friends* first—"

"Thank you for explaining. For being honest. I get it, how it can feel to be lonely. I guess I'm thrown off because . . . I'm not sure if this is a sign or something."

"A sign?" I say incredulously. "A sign of what?"

"That maybe this isn't a good idea." He's talking about *us*. Us being together. Dread grips my core, suffocating my thoughts.

"I don't know what to say," I mumble. "I mean, me being honest with you is a sign of how I feel about you. I thought you . . . liked me."

"I do, Naina. I really do. I guess I'm just . . . hurt," he says.

I drop my forehead into my hands. I know I had to tell him the truth, but I had dared to hope for a different response.

"I am hurt, and I don't know, maybe we should pause, take a step back, reevaluate." He gulps down his water.

Something begins to stir in me, turbulent and explosive, rising through my chest and buzzing through my fingertips.

"You're such a fuckboy," I respond, cold and exasperated.

"Naina . . . what?" David laughs uncomfortably. I savor his reaction, the control I feel from eliciting it.

"You're a fuckboy. You flirted with me, you made me feel something, then you slept with me and went on a trip, and I didn't hear from you. Once. And of course I felt horrible, so I did something fucking human—and, fine, *stupid*—and tried to fill the void, and now you're using this as an excuse to say we should stop, but in reality, it's just that—an excuse. You just want this to end without looking like the bad guy. So now I'm the bad guy? Because you went dark on me?"

The words fly out of my mouth, spit collecting at the sides of my lips. My heart pulsates against my chest, my blood hot in my ears.

"Naina . . . none of that is true. I'm sorry, but it isn't, and you know it," David finally says after a moment of painful silence.

"Really? Because that's exactly how it looks. That's *what happened*," I retort, refusing to back down.

"*No*," he presses on cautiously, lowering his voice against mine. "That's the story you're choosing to tell yourself to deal with the pain."

I scoff. "Pain? This isn't pain. It's anger."

"Well, I feel pain," David says. "Because I did—*I do*—feel something for you. I don't want this to end. I'm hurt. I know we aren't exclusive—we didn't talk about it—but fuck. Your ex. The only person you've ever been with. When I suggested that we take it slow and see how it feels, I meant just that. Only that." David throws his hands up, helpless. He steadies himself by clasping his fingers together. "I feel for you and what you're going through with your ex. I don't want to muck up your—your progress."

"I'm being honest, David. I'm telling you what happened between Sofia and me. Which *is* progress," I explain. "I'm being vulnerable with you, and it feels like you're just giving up!"

David looks at me from beneath the shadow of his brow, observing me with what seems to be sympathy or perhaps pity. I can't stand it. Then he clears his throat.

"I know this is hard for you," he says, his voice solid and sharp. "But I'm not a—a *fuckboy*." The word sounds so strange coming from his mouth. I immediately know I mislabeled him.

"I'm trying to be intentional. I have feelings for you," David continues. "It's a lot for me to process—to go from being your friend, to almost having you, to this. I know it must have been weird to not hear from me, and I'm sorry it hurt you, but . . . I'm allowed to be *more* hurt you slept with your ex, okay?" David throws his hands up. "Fuck, Naina, doesn't being hurt prove that I care?"

"It does," I huff.

"I don't want this to end," he replies. "I don't."

"I realize telling you I slept with my ex is an unortho-dox way of showing it," I say. "But this is me trying."

"I know," he says, exhaling. He places his hand on my knee. "And, look, I know I need to try, too. I didn't mean what I said earlier, about this being a sign or something. I'm just . . . I don't know. Scared. I haven't had many relationships that have felt this real." He turns away from me. "Any." He sighs.

My mind races, searching for a way to respond. Con-ceding might be the only way to move forward. "Maybe we both said mean, dumb things." I touch his wrist. "The fuckboy comment was wrong, I know. But, look at us, we're already working through it."

David gives me a half smile.

"I know you are hurt and that it's my fault," I tell him. "I'm really sorry. But I am attempting—unsuccessfully—to explain to you how seeing Sofia made clear how much I want to be with *you*. I told her about us."

"What did you tell her?" he asks, now holding my fingers in his hand, stroking them with his thumb.

"That I have feelings for you. That we slept together. That we started out as friends but that, for me, it has become so much more than that."

"That must have been hard for her," he says softly, with

compassion. I lean off the barstool and throw my arms around his shoulders.

It is one thing to own up to my mistakes; it is another to ask for forgiveness. It's a level of vulnerability I've resisted for years, but in this moment with David, it's suddenly the only thing I can do.

"You are a good person, David," I whisper in his ear. "I am sorry I slept with her. I am sorry I hurt you. I am sorry I called you a fuckboy. I am sorry. I'm *so* sorry."

He wraps his arms around my lower back. "I need some time to think about us." He pulls away. "Maybe you could use the time too? Is that okay?"

I am threatened by this suggestion. I'm only just recovering from the ache of not hearing from him. Now he wants to go *back* to not speaking to each other?

"For how long?" I ask.

He pinches my chin between his thumb and forefinger. "Five days," he replies. "How is that?"

"That is a very long time." I feel petulant and young when I say it.

David laughs with his chest and pats my knee. I rest my chin on my hand, already dreading the silence between us.

"I should leave," David says. "I hate sitting in wet clothes."

"I'll walk out with you."

I want to be wrapped up in him, to immerse myself in the certainty of what I feel for him. Instead, we put on our jackets and leave the bar. We hug goodbye and walk in opposite directions.

Here it is again: the loss of control. I tried to eradicate uncertainty from my life; I spiraled against it. Now I've only generated more of it. I was too late in admitting what I wanted, in admitting that I was at fault, in recovering from it all.

Perhaps what I am receiving, and what I've received my entire adult life thus far, is my reflection flung back at me.

XII

Three days later, some good news unexpectedly finds its way to me: My essay will be published.

Fresh out of the shower, wet hair dripping down my back and shoulders, I blink profusely and rub my eyes before rereading the email, desperate to savor every word. There will be some light edits, the pay is modest but sufficient, and I'll have my first byline by the new year. My words will be in both digital and print form, in a publication that I actually read. I thank myself for trying, for putting myself out there. I cringe at myself for embracing cringe.

The essay emphasizes the online preservation of the worst parts of ourselves. Strangers arrive at collective verdicts about who we are based on our worst moments, if we're unlucky enough. When our mistakes are put on blast, it's a challenge to not be defined by them. If the love bomber changed, healed, found authenticity in his relationships, the internet would not care. Truth expands and morphs; what was true of him at one point might no longer be true in the future. To some people, he would always be the love bomber. He would have to be okay with that.

I wrap myself in a towel and walk to my bedroom, creating a damp spot on my comforter as I sit down to text my father and Jordan the news. I'm tempted to share the update with David, but I know I shouldn't. I still have two days left of my sentence to serve. I leave my phone under my pillow, turning my notifications off, forcing the option out of my mind.

Seventy-something hours without speaking to David or knowing where we stand feels stretched into an eternity. I went to a show last night hoping to see him but ended up running into Christian instead. We ate pizza while perched on the sidewalk curb, grease dripping onto the concrete.

"How's David?" I asked him as nonchalantly as I could manage.

"I don't know," Christian said, chewing thoughtfully. "He's never home."

"Oh."

"Yeah, I think he's helping a friend with a shoot or something."

"Oh."

"You guys not talking?"

I rolled my eyes, feigning indifference. "We're taking a break."

"Ah."

Though Christian and I had discussed our relationship history extensively and shamelessly, talking about my situation with David was a different endeavor.

"It'll blow over," Christian said, stuffing the last bit of crust into his mouth and rubbing his hands together. "These things always do."

"What," I retorted, "so now I'm just another number in the endless stream of women? Statistically, these things blow over?"

Christian raised his hands, surrendering, eyes wide from the blow of my bitterness.

"I'm just sad, is all," I said. "I like him."

"When things get complicated, isn't it better to take a step back?" Christian posed. "It's like staring at a painting too close or something, then you don't get the full picture."

"That's, like, very astute Christian."

"David likes you too," he said. "I think he's just trying to do things differently this time around."

I immediately mentally dissected his words, searching for clues as to what David might be thinking. I pocketed the knowledge of Christian knowing how David feels about me. But what does that mean, doing things differently? Can that even be possible, to alter your intentions when you catch yourself in a pattern, if all the ingredients for behavioral disaster are already present? At what point can you stop and tell yourself it will be different this time and make it so?

I am afraid I will always stand too close to the thought of David.

Jhanaki notices a shift in my mood, and she invites me to a club with a group of her friends.

"A *club*? I didn't know you went out." I look at her aghast.

"Quarterly. Don't be weird about it."

I take Molly at someone's pregame festivities. I think of David while mixing the powder into a glass of water.

"Did you test this?" I ask Jhanaki. She glances sheepishly at her friend with bleached eyebrows, the supplier of the Molly (amongst other things). Eyebrows shrugs nonchalantly.

"Dangerous," I murmur, gulping the water. I feel reckless, looking for any exit from purgatory.

"She just hooked up with her ex-girlfriend," Jhanaki explains to Eyebrows. "And she was ghosted by a guy she was fucking."

"He didn't ghost me," I respond, considering a hit of the joint Jhanaki is holding while Eyebrows squints at me. "I mean, it felt like he did, but he was away on a trip and didn't have service. And while he was gone, my ex-girlfriend showed up. Then I had to *actually* end things with her, for good. Then he came back and I had to tell him about seeing my ex and now we are on a break."

Eyebrows curls their lip and shakes their head empathically.

"Our bi queen," Jhanaki says, placing her arm around my shoulders and shaking me affectionately.

The next morning, Sunday, I wake up at 1 p.m., feeling like all the joy has been sucked out of me. I don't regret the Molly or the night out—they were conscious choices I made—but I have to find less exhausting or reckless ways to satisfy my need for control.

In some kind of effort to erase myself and thus erase whatever I'm feeling, I deactivate my social media accounts. I think of the love bomber.

bitch, Jordan texts me an hour or so later, *did you delete your Instagram?*

I silence my phone notifications, once again, as if to train my mind against the delusional urge to check if David has texted me. Part of me clings to the hope he'll break his own rule.

I can't stand the thought of work tomorrow. Of the promise of the new week and its fresh start. I hear Jhanaki washing dishes in the living room, and although I'm tempted to debrief last night's activities with her, my serotonin levels feel dangerously low to be good company.

You need to be nice to yourself. My mother had said this to me when I was a kid, my father later absorbing it into his own philosophy to cope with his grief. He'd remind me of this often via text when I'd complain about being too lazy to cook or clean my apartment. He said it to me when he dropped me off at the airport the day I left for New York.

I recognize what I am feeling: grief. Over Sofia, over

a lost chance with David, over a version of myself that no longer exists. It seems dramatic, because I know I'll be okay, and no one's *dead*. I know what *that* feels like, the permanence of it, and it's incomparable—yet the ache of this feeling is the same.

XIII

On my fifth day of not speaking to David, Chloe rushes to my desk, forehead creased.

"Naina, we need to go *now*," she says, reaching for my chair and spinning it away from my computer. "Where's your bag? Grab it. Let's go."

"Chloe, what the fuck," I respond, clumsily dropping my phone. "What's going on?"

"David just *called me*," she says. "He says he couldn't reach you. Christian got into a bike accident. He says he's going to be okay, but David sounds . . . not okay. We need to *go*."

We approach Alice, who is battling a cold and blowing her nose into a tissue. "Alice," Chloe says, "our friend is in the hospital. We need to leave right now."

"I'm so sorry," she says, sniffling. "Both of you?"

"Yes," Chloe says. "So, we're going now, okay?"

"All right," Alice responds, turning away from us. "As long as your work is finished."

"It's not," Chloe says. "But our friend is in the hospital, so we'll finish it later."

Alice shrugs. "All right."

"What a bitch," I say while Chloe calls us a car in the elevator. I'm restless now, spewing a million questions: How badly is Christian hurt? What did David sound like on the phone? How long ago did it happen? How far is this hospital?

The weary nurse at the emergency room reception says only one of us can go in. Wordlessly, Chloe sits down in the waiting room and gestures toward me. My restlessness morphs into hesitation—I can't stand hospitals, the smell of them, the sound of patients in pain, the dodging of gurneys. I sanitize my hands, applying more pressure than I need to. I take a moment to collect myself. Then I begin my search for Christian and David.

I get lost in a maze of beeping machines and cubbylike rooms. Doctors and family members are too absorbed by their duties and tragedies to notice me circling around helplessly. I actively push thoughts of previous visits to halls like these out of my mind. I know I need to find my friends soon, before my brain jumps the track. I make eye contact with a woman stressfully dabbing at her wet, flushed cheeks. Realizing I've passed by her four times now, I finally give up and call David. He answers on the first ring.

"Naina," he says, "are you here?"

"Yes, but I can't find you."

"Walk straight from reception. We're last on the right."

I trace my footsteps back until I find David's back poking out from behind a curtain, the left side of his body leaning against the wall. I say his name, and he shoots up, pushing the curtain open. His eyes are pink and puffy. Christian is a lump under layers of sheets, nose pointing toward the ceiling.

David pulls me into him. "Christian, Naina's here," he says, still embracing me. Christian waves. "Hi, Naina," he says weakly. "Thanks for coming."

"I'm so glad you're talking and that you're okay, Christian," I say, leaning over him. "Or that you seem okay?"

"He will be. Right, Christian? Rana is on her way, too." David pats Christian's leg. My heart swells at David's tenderness toward his best friend and the relief of hearing Christian speak.

"Chloe brought me here," I tell them. "She's in the waiting room. Only two people at a time."

David nods. "I drove here," he says. "Christian's car. He called me from the ambulance."

Christian smiles and looks back up at the ceiling. I motion for David to step outside of the room, and he does, closing the curtain.

"What happened?" I whisper. Christian starts to explain, but David interjects, urging him to rest. He explains that Christian was leaving work early, biking home, when a car turned into him and knocked him off his cycle. His shoulder is probably broken. Luckily, he was wearing a helmet—he'd learned his lesson from the last time he fell—but he will need a CT scan. They're waiting on X-rays.

David exhales a gust of air and shakes his head, placing his hands over his eyes. "The doctor told me that car and bike accidents go up by 20 percent during the winter," he whispers. "I know I'm not the one who got hit, but I think I am about to lose it. I need a Xanax or something."

I rub David's left forearm. His sweatshirt is bunched up at his elbows. I think about him driving Christian's car, making his cautious turns, double-checking the mirrors, keeping the music low to concentrate.

"You're allowed to not be okay," I reply. "I know what this is like."

He chuckles, like he can't deal with himself right now, and tears stream down his face. I hug him, hard, my head pressing against his chest. My own anxiety at being here melds with gratitude that I can be here with him, that I can bring him comfort.

"I'll be okay," he says, pulling away. "I'm just emotional. It's not about me. I don't want to have an anxiety attack when Christian needs me. And anyway, the hospital staff needs me to save them from Christian."

"I can hear everything you're saying," Christian calls from behind the curtain.

David rolls his eyes. "You need more drugs or something," he calls back. "You should be asleep."

"Do you know when my parents will be here?"

"They're on their way. Driving down right now," David says.

"My mom is going to be so pissed at me. She hates that I bike in the city."

"She won't be pissed," I respond, pulling the curtain back open. "She's going to be so relieved. And then maybe later she'll be a little pissed, but you don't need to worry about that."

David and I sit back down to talk to Christian, hoping to bring some levity to the moment. He's on painkillers, mostly ibuprofen, despite begging the doctor for Vicodin. I distract him with a rant about Alice, specifically her annoyance that I had to leave work for an emergency.

"I honestly think she needs to go on a date. Or make a friend," I say. "That might put her in a good mood."

"Is she cute?" Christian asks. I shrug. "Once I'm better . . . I got you. Put me in the same room as her, and I'll take care of the rest." He gives me a thumbs-up with his good arm but still winces as he moves it.

"The meds are affecting your judgment," David says.

After an hour of us attempting to pass the time, a doctor appears with the X-ray results. Christian has indeed broken his shoulder, in three places. Christian stares catatonically as he absorbs this information, our small dose of humor draining away. The doctor leaves just as quickly as he arrived. David turns to Christian, apologetic.

"Your parents will be here in thirty minutes or so," David says, checking his phone. The curtain flies open, and Chloe appears this time.

"I snuck in," she says, shrugging at me. She sits on the edge of Christian's bed and squeezes his ankle. "I'm so glad you're alive," she whispers.

"Me too," Christian says, cocking his head to the side. "You're so pretty."

Chloe places a hand on her chest, endeared by Christian's still intact charisma.

David's leaning his head against the wall, eyes closed, seemingly taking deep breaths. I exchange a glance with Chloe, who gives me a consolatory nod. "Go," she mouths, making a shooing motion with her hands.

"Christian, how about I spend some time with you until your parents get here," Chloe says, smoothing the sheets. Christian looks at David, then me, then smiles at Chloe.

"David, can I drive you home?" I ask.

David shrugs weakly, eyes still closed.

"Thank you for coming here," Christian tells him. "I know hospitals are tough for you. I needed you and you came. I love you."

David opens his eyes, tears running down his cheeks again. He stands up to pat Christian's knee.

"I was excited to finally call you today," David murmurs, his head in his hands. "And then this happened."

I'm driving Christian's car, focusing closely on this job I've given myself to get David home safely. I haven't driven since I left Chicago and have always hated being behind the wheel. I didn't tell David this, though. When we exited the hospital, I held my palm open, and he placed Christian's keys in it.

"Life is boring and mundane until it's not," I respond. David doesn't say anything to this. He's looking out the window.

"I wish I wasn't like this," he says with a sigh, mostly talking to himself. "I should be able to be there for him. What happened in high school—that was such a long time ago."

"You were, though," I insist. "There for him. You spent nearly three hours at the hospital. You called his parents and his friends so he'd have his support system around him." I want to look at him, but I keep my eyes straight ahead. "David, what happened to—you were retraumatized. I know how you feel, at least a little, because I feel it every time I walk into a hospital. It's a lot."

He shakes his head. "I feel weak," he mumbles. "Really fucking weak."

"You are *not* weak. You showed up for Christian."

"So did you."

"I did. But I also showed up for you." I feel David's hand come to my knee as he tilts his head back into the headrest and turns his face toward me.

"Thank you, Naina. You're the only person I wanted."

Nearly an hour later, we're back in Brooklyn. After multiple frustrating attempts, I manage to park the car. David trudges toward his apartment. I follow closely behind him, sympathetic toward this side of him.

Inside, he collapses on the couch, furling into a fetal position. I go through his fridge and cupboards.

"What're you doing?" he mumbles sleepily.

"It's almost eight," I say. "We should eat something."

He grumbles in response as I take stock of ingredients, dig around for a cutting board, and preheat the oven. While tomatoes, onion, and garlic roast, I walk over to the couch and sit next to David, his large body curled up like a little boy's.

I tousle his hair gently, and he stirs, looking up at me.

"I'm making tomato soup," I say. "And grilled cheese."

He releases a groggy sound. "You're cooking for me," he says.

"Of course," I say, tugging at his hair between my fingers.

"Tell me something good," he begs. "Please. I need to be distracted."

"Well," I say, "my essay is going to be published."

David looks up at me, his face upside down. "Naina," he says, "that is the best thing I've heard all week. Who's publishing it? When will it come out?"

I tell him the details, and he listens closely, his puffy eyes now growing wide with supportive excitement.

"I'm so happy for you," he says.

"Thank you. And thank you for helping me, for being there for me," I say.

David turns onto his back and shifts his weight to rest his head on my thigh, his hands clasped across his chest. "I want to be there for you," he whispers. "I know I asked for time to think. And I guess I did—think. I mostly just couldn't stop thinking about you. Wishing I was with you. I need you."

I run a finger up and down the length of his nose, and he closes his eyes, exhaling.

"I'm here, aren't I?" I ask. He nods.

"I think I got caught up in this myth," he says after a few minutes.

"What myth?"

"That you have to wait to be some ideal version of yourself before you go after what you want. Like growth can't happen alongside it, or even because of it. I guess I felt like we needed to wait until conditions were perfect—for both of us—to pursue anything. But I'm realizing the whole point is that the conditions improve when we're together." He is quiet again, but just for a moment. "And I'd like to be together."

The combination of relief and clarity I feel at hearing him say this renders me momentarily speechless. I want to grow into a better version of myself, but I want to do that with David. I am tired of trying to control the terms of being human: when I will get hurt or cause hurt. It's an impossible balancing act, and I can't do it while being fair to him or myself. That's the inherent risk of loving others. I've been too stubborn to accept it.

"I do too," I say. "And I choose you because you're imperfect. And so am I."

David's eyes flutter open to meet mine. I lean over to

kiss him at the corner of his mouth, tasting the salt from his tears.

"We're going to be okay," I tell him. "We all are."

"I know," he replies. "But you and me especially." He reaches for my body, his arms stretching over his head.

"Come here," he says. "Come home." I move toward him, tears pooling in my eyes, clouding my vision as they fall. Something inside of me slowly expands, stretching like a rubber band. I shut my eyelids as my face finds its rightful place in the crook of his neck.

This book is over, but you can still spend time with Naina and David. See how their story continues to unfold in the epilogue, get the ingredients for their pasta night, and experience David's scent in candle form. Scan here or visit 831stories.com/comedictiming.

ACKNOWLEDGMENTS

For regenerating the hopeless romantic in me and bringing this book to life, I'm indebted to Erica Cerulo and Claire Mazur of 831 Stories.

For editorial insights that illuminated the power and finesse of romance books, thanks to Jennifer Prokop and Sanjana Basker.

For indispensable love, support, and inspiration, I am grateful to Risha Sona, Nicolas Sessler, Nirmala Penmasta, Jasmine Newson, Alexis Godfrey, and Alyssa Anchelowitz.

ABOUT THE AUTHOR

UPASNA BARATH is a writer and performer who grew up in India and the US. She was a contributor to *Rookie Mag* and a Steppenwolf Theatre Literary Fellow. She lives in Brooklyn, New York.